Least Wanted

Also by

Debbi Mack

Identity Crisis

Five Uneasy Pieces

Least Wanted

Debbi Mack

Renegade Press

Savage, MD

Renegade Press
P.O. Box 156
Savage, MD

Library of Congress Cataloging-in-Publication Data
Least Wanted by Debbi Mack
    ISBN: 978-0-9829508-1-4
    Library of Congress Control Number: 2010913536

DEDICATION

For Joyce and Andrew Mack, my parents, who instilled a love of reading and stories in me early on and always encouraged me to pursue my dreams.

And for Rick Iacangelo, my husband, who's believed in me all along and been an endless source of support and inspiration during the toughest of times.

ACKNOWLEDGMENTS

My writing career has been an adventure, in every possible sense of the word. I feel incredibly grateful to have been helped by many people along the way. My current writers' group has contributed so much, in terms of suggestions, constructive criticism and overall support, that I want to thank all the members (past and present), including Janet Benrey, Ray Flynt, Sasscer Hill, Mary Ellen Hughes, Trish Marshall, Sherriell Mattingley, Bonnie Settle, Thomas Sprenkle, Marcia Talley, and Lyn Taylor. You all have been an invaluable aid to my growth as a writer. I also owe a great debt of gratitude to Pat Altner, Jack Bludis, Carla Buckley, Carolyn Males, Ellen Rawlings, Louise Titchener, and other writers and friends who provided helpful suggestions and encouragement along the way.

I'd like to thank Paul Lenharr, the (now retired) intake counselor at the Prince George's County State's Attorney's Office for his helpful information about girl gangs and juvenile crime in the county. I'd also like to thank Jennifer Ferrara, a public high school guidance counselor, who educated me about release requirements for school disciplinary records. In addition, my thanks go to Rick Maltz, a certified fraud examiner, who kept me straight on the embezzlement and auditing details. Any errors or omissions on these subjects are my own. My endless thanks to Peter Ratcliffe for doing an exemplary job on the cover art, along with Beth Rubin for her awesome editing and my sister, Nancy, for her thoughtful (and eagle-eyed) critique. A special shout out goes to my friends in the Chesapeake Chapter of Sisters in Crime, as well as to Laurie Cullen, for copyediting and helping this techno-idiot with the formatting.

CHAPTER ONE

Shanae Jackson breezed into my office like she owned the place. Not even a knock or word of greeting. Pint-sized and wiry, in jeans and a plain orange T-shirt, Shanae projected an attitude that compensated for her lack of stature.

Her daughter, Tina, trailed behind her. Though she was quite tall for a 13-year-old—taller by a couple of inches than her mother—she slouched as if standing up straight carried too much responsibility. Tina slumped into a chair and began reading a book, while Shanae took the other seat and glared at me.

"Hi," I said, hurriedly closing out the online research I'd been doing. "You must be Shanae Jackson."

"You got someone else you meetin' at two o'clock today?" she asked. Her piercing brown-eyed gaze pinned me to my chair.

"Um, no."

"Then I guess I must be." She spoke in a tone reserved for the village idiot.

I plastered on a big smile and refrained from telling her to fuck off. Standing and extending my hand, I said, "I'm Sam McRae. It's nice to meet you."

I half expected another snappy comeback, but she remained seated, looking at my hand like I'd just blown my nose into it. After a moment, she reached out and grasped my fingers.

I risked further sarcasm and turned to the girl. "And you must be Tina. Hi."

Tina glanced at me. "Hey," she said, then glued her eyes back on the book.

In contrast to Tina's slouch, Shanae sat bolt upright, her posture as intense as her gaze. Her abundant hair was plastered back from a dark chocolate face with high cheekbones and angular lines.

I sat down and opened the thin file containing notes of my earlier phone conversation with the angry woman sitting before me.

"Is that the paperwork?" I asked, nodding toward an envelope clutched in her left hand.

Shanae thrust it at me. I pulled out folded copies of the police report and other papers concerning her daughter's case. Smoothing them out on my desk, I took some time to review them.

"This looks pretty straightforward," I said. "As I mentioned on the phone, I'll need to speak to your daughter alone."

I wouldn't have thought it possible, but Shanae's expression hardened.

"I gots to stay," she said. "I'm her mother."

"Tina is my client. I have to discuss the case with her alone."

"But I'm her mother," she said.

I suppressed a sigh. In juvenile cases, it's never easy to explain to parents the need for complete attorney-client confidentiality. From the moment I saw her, I knew Shanae Jackson would be no exception.

"I have an ethical duty to keep client confidences," I said. "Things Tina and I say in front of you are no longer confidential."

"But I'm her *mother*." She stressed the last word, as if I hadn't heard it the first two times. Shooting a withering look at Tina, she slapped the girl's arm. "Put that book down, child!" With a grimace, Tina closed the book and set it on her lap.

"In the eyes of the law, you're another person. I have to ask you to leave."

"I'll find another lawyer," she said, her eyes filled with accusations of my shortcomings.

"You can *ask* the Public Defender for the name of another lawyer who'll do this for a reduced fee, but whoever you get will tell you the same thing."

Still glaring at me, Shanae kept silent. If she thought that look would force me to change my mind, the woman knew nothing about me. Or maybe she resented the fact that, while she was too well-off to get a public defender, one glance at my dinky sublet office and she could see I was no Gloria Allred. I was just another scrambling solo who took work from the public defender's short list of private attorneys willing to represent defendants on the financial borderline.

"White people," she said, for no apparent reason.

I didn't know if she was smitten with her own voice or blamed white people for her lot in life, the rules of professional conduct, or the price of gas. Maybe she was disappointed at my color. For the pittance I stood to earn from this case, I was ready to tell her to find a black attorney.

I considered telling her about my childhood in the Bed-Stuy section of Brooklyn or pointing to the wall behind her at my father's photo of Jackie Robinson entering the Dodgers clubhouse through the door marked "KEEP OUT." Not so much to impress her, but to clue her in that she didn't know jack shit about me.

She grumbled, "This is bullshit."

I yanked open the bottom drawer of my old wooden desk and hauled out my Yellow Pages, dropping it, with an intentional thud, in front of her. "Here you go," I said, flipping to the attorney listings. "Call anyone. And be prepared to pay dearly for what they have to say."

She pursed her lips and continued to give me the evil eye. But she knew I had her. "Fine," she said. Grabbing the large black purse she'd parked next to her, she shot to her feet as if the chair were on fire. "I need to do some shopping," she announced.

I nodded and smiled, like I gave a damn where she was going or what she intended to do. "This shouldn't take more than an hour."

"Hmmph." She turned toward Tina. In a stern voice, she said, "You behave. And answer Ms. McRae's questions, you hear me?" Over her shoulder on her way out, she tossed the words, "I'll be back."

Goody, I thought. Tina's sullen expression suggested our thoughts were identical.

Sinking into the chair like a deflating balloon, Tina's elbows jutted over the armrests as she crossed her arms. Her blue-jeaned legs waggled, signaling boredom. I could see the outline of rail-thin arms and bony shoulders under the loose-fitting pink sweatshirt that swallowed her frame. She must have taken after her father. Her chubby-cheeked face and café au lait complexion were nothing like her mother's. Her hair was tied in a ponytail with a pink sequined scrunchie.

"Tina, it says here you knocked an elderly woman down while trying to snatch her purse. Is that right?"

She shrugged. "Yeah." Her look said, "What about it?"

"Based on what I have, this looks like your first offense. What brought this on?"

She shrugged again. "I just tried to jack her purse," she said, revealing a crooked overbite. "She wouldn't let go."

"Why did you do it?"

She rolled her eyes. At least her repertoire included more than shrugging. "Why you think?" she said, in a tone that suggested I might be missing a few brain cells.

"I could assume lots of things, but I'm asking you."

Again, she shrugged. "Money, I guess."

"You guess?"

"Money," she said, in a flat voice.

"How much money did you expect to find in an old lady's purse?"

Shrug. I suppressed the urge to hold her shoulders down. "I dunno," she mumbled.

I scanned the report again. "This happened three blocks from where you live. Do you know this woman?"

She shook her head.

"You have a problem with her?"

Silence.

"You just figured you had nothing better to do, so why not pick up some spare change from a little old lady who can't defend herself?"

Tina shrugged and rolled her eyes. "Whatever."

"Was breaking her arm part of the plan?"

Some emotion—regret?—flashed in her eyes, but her game face returned quickly. "I wasn't tryin' to knock her down. If she'd let go the damn purse, she'd o' been all right."

"But she didn't let go. And you got caught." A pair of undercover cops sitting surveillance had intervened when they heard the woman scream.

"Yeah. Jump out boys got me," she said. "Motherfuckers."

"Jump out boys?"

"You know. Unmarked."

I nodded. You learn something new every day. "What are your grades like?" I asked, switching gears.

"Okay, I guess."

I went through the tedious process of digging for more information. Bottom line: she was an average student who read at a higher-than-average grade level. And she had better verbal abilities than her terse responses would suggest.

"So what're you reading now?" I asked.

She held up the book. *A Piece of Cake* by Cupcake Brown.

"I read that. Quite a story."

She nodded. "It's real."

It was real, all right. The memoir was a mature selection for a 13-year-old girl. Cupcake Brown (her real name) had run away from a dreadful foster home and ended up in a gang, addicted to drugs—before her eighteenth birthday. She hit rock bottom, living in a dumpster at one point. With some support from other recovering addicts and the law firm that employed her, Cupcake turned it all around and became an attorney. An uplifting story about possibilities that casts a positive light on lawyers—and you don't get to hear many of those.

"Are you reading that for class?"

"Naw. Jus' for fun."

"It's refreshing to meet a young person who reads." I winced at my choice of words, those of an old fart. Tina didn't seem to notice. "You do any after-school stuff?" I asked.

"I played softball up 'til last year, but I dropped outta that."

"How come?"

Another shrug. Maybe she was trying to work out knots in her shoulders. "I dunno. Just don't feel like it no more."

"Ever do any volunteer work?"

She shook her head.

"Go to church?"

Negative.

"Your mom go to church?"

"Naw. She work Sundays."

I was fishing for the kind of "give-her-a-break-your-Honor-she's-a-good-kid-with-a-bright-future" stuff that defense attorneys routinely trot out, in the hope their clients will get off with lighter sentences. Unfortunately, this approach tended to work better for middle-class kids who had been fast-tracked for success as early as nursery school. By high school, they were already padding their future résumés with internships and other extracurricular activities that would set them apart from—or at least keep them abreast of—their career-driven peers. Unfortunately, the neighborhoods that fed Silver Hill Middle School were far from middle-class, and many of the students were busier building rap sheets than résumés. So the "bright, shiny future" stuff seemed less workable than the "let's-not-make-things-any-worse-than-they-have-to-be" approach.

With that in mind, I asked, "Have you ever been suspended?"

"Nuh-uh. I done some detentions."

"What for?"

"Bein' late, talking in class." She ticked them off on her fingers. "Once for getting in a fight, but the other girl started it."

I looked at her. She stared back, daring me to say otherwise. "How'd it start?"

"I was eating lunch in the caf with my friends. This heifer named Lakeesha, she step up, start dissin' my friend, Rochelle. She always raggin' on her. She jus' jealous, is all. Anyway, she start in on Rochelle again. Rochelle say, 'Girl, you got a mouth on you. You want to back your noise with some action?'"

Tina snickered. "That heifer was frontin', big time. She back down. I kep' a eye on her, anyway.

"Then, when we was getting up to leave, Lakeesha get up, too. I saw her come up behind Rochelle wit' a razor in her hand. So I shoved Lakeesha and knocked her ass down. Then Rochelle and this other girl start wailin' on the bitch for sneakin' up on her like that. I started kickin' her, too."

"So you were the one who knocked her down?" *Just like the old woman with the purse.* "Why were you kicking her, if she was already down?" *And would you have beaten up the old lady if the cops hadn't been there?*

"Lakeesha the one wit' the razor," she said, in a soft voice. "I couldn't just let her try to cut Rochelle up and get away with it."

Sounded reasonable, assuming it was the truth, and you could never be sure about that. But if Tina were going to lie to me, why mention the fight at all? I'd represented a handful of violent juveniles—all boys. They'd had more attitude than brains. Tina didn't seem to fit that profile, even if she did talk tough. Or maybe I was letting her gender, baby face, and slightly nerdy overbite fool me.

"Have you been in fights before?" I asked.

"No. But I ain't scared to fight or nothin'." Her voice took on a petulant, defensive tone.

"Well, no one said you were, but I'd avoid it, if I were you." What was with the attitude? Maybe someone accused her of being chicken. Maybe she'd gone after the old woman on a dare. "You can be suspended for fighting at school, you know. Or even expelled. I guess they cut you a break because you were defending your friend."

"That an', like I say, I ain't never been in no fight before. Mr. Powell, he put in a good word for me, too."

"Who's Mr. Powell?"

"Guidance counselor."

I finished up our interview with some routine questions, a brief description of juvenile court and the probable outcome in her case. I suspected that, as a first-time offender, the court would go easy on Tina, but I qualified every possible result with "maybe," because you never know for sure.

When we'd finished the formalities, I said, "I loved to read when I was your age. Seems like I hardly have the time now. What else have you read?"

"*I Know Why the Caged Bird Sings.*"

"Maya Angelou. I read that, too." *In high school.* She wasn't lacking in intellect.

Tina's face remained impassive, but her eyes warmed to the subject of books. "I also read *Coldest Winter Ever* by Sister Souljah." She gave me a speculative look. "Whatchoo read when you was a kid?"

"Lots of books." I tried to think back. Seemed like a century ago, though it was closer to a quarter of that. "*Catcher in the Rye. A Tree Grows in Brooklyn.*"

"I think we s'posed to read that *Catcher* book in high school. Don't know the other one."

"They may not teach it. I guess I liked it because I'm from Brooklyn."

"Oh, yeah? I got a uncle live in Brooklyn. In Bed-Stuy."

"That's where I'm from."

Her eyes narrowed into a quizzical squint. "But ain't that mostly black?"

"Yes, it is. And it was when I was there, too." That was in the 1970s, not the best of times for Bedford-Stuyvesant, once known as the biggest ghetto in the U.S. Not the best place for a pale-skinned white girl like me to be living, either.

Her expression was appraising now, as if trying to gauge exactly who I was in light of this new information. I must have passed some test, because her expression softened and she smiled.

I gave Tina my card which she stuck in her book.

"Call me anytime, if you have questions. Or want to talk about books."

"Okay, Ms. McRae."

"Call me Sam."

Three raps on the door and Shanae poked her head in. I checked my watch. She'd been away an hour, to the minute.

"You done, right?" she said. "I need to talk to you." To Tina, she said, "Go downstairs and wait," dismissing her with a wave of her hand.

The animation drained from Tina's expression as she rose. Glaring at her mother, she slunk out and closed the door.

Shanae shook her head. "That girl trouble. She need to clean up her act, you see what I'm sayin'?"

"She's at that age, I guess."

"Yeah, and I don't know how much longer she gonna live, if she keep up her bullshit."

"Well, this is her first offense, so to speak. It should go pretty smoothly. It may take a month or two before we get a hearing before a master. A master is like a junior judge—"

Shanae dipped her chin, in a brief nod. "Fine," she said. "You jus' let me know when her court date is. I gots another problem to talk to you about."

I was surprised she didn't have more questions about Tina's situation, since she'd been so adamant about staying for the interview. "What is it?"

"You do child support cases?" she asked, taking the seat she'd vacated an hour before.

"Yes."

"I need a lawyer," she said. "My girl's father owe me child support. I wanna do sumpin' 'bout it."

"I'd be happy to help you," I said, doubting my own words. There was no conflict of interest that I could see. And I could always use the work. "I would have to charge my regular fee, though."

I thought that might end the discussion. "I can work that out," she said. "My brother'll lend me the money."

"Okay," I said. I wondered if she'd discussed it with her brother and why she hadn't asked him for help when she failed to qualify for public defender services. I decided to get some case particulars, since I always give an initial free consult.

According to Shanae, Rodney Fisher had acknowledged paternity of Tina a few years after she was born, though he and Shanae had never married. He'd paid child support, not always regularly, since then. Shanae said he was making more money now and she wanted to sue for past-due support and seek an increase in his monthly obligation.

10

"Rodney making way more money than he say he does."
A worldly-wise smirk creased her face. "Under-the-table
money, you see what I'm sayin'?"

"I get your drift. How do you know this? Off-the-books
earnings can be difficult, if not impossible, to prove."

"I got a friend been looking into this. He can tell you. See,
Rodney own a pawn shop. I think a lot of money coming in
that ain't making it onto the books. Unnerstan?"

"I'd like to talk to your friend," I said. "And see any
documentation you have on his income, along with a copy of
the child support order."

"Oh, I can get that for you. Make me sick. I had to take
another job, since Giant cut back my hours. Sons of bitches.
And that worthless niggah think he can screw me outta my
child support. Well, we'll just see 'bout that."

"As we discussed, it'll be three hundred dollars to handle
your daughter's case. For your case, I'll have to ask for a two
thousand dollar retainer up front," I said. "If the retainer's
used up, I'll bill you monthly. I need payment by cashier's
check or money order."

Without batting an eye, she said, "Okay." I gritted my
teeth thinking about this woman's temerity to go poor-
mouthing for a referral from the public defender's office.
Should have asked for four grand on the child support case.

I pulled up the retainer agreement for Tina's case and a
release form to get access to her school information. I also
opened a standard form for Shanae's case, and typed in the
retainer amount before printing the papers.

I told her to read them over and invited her to ask
questions. She read and signed them without comment. Just
to be sure, I reviewed the main terms with her. Shanae
handed me a $300 money order for Tina's case. Seeing that
she had come with payment in hand made me feel better.

"I'll start work on your child support case after I get the
two thousand dollars," I reminded Shanae. I made copies of

the retainer agreement for her and her brother and handed her another business card.

"All right. Thank you, Ms. McRae."

Her sudden politeness was a welcome change. "Call me Sam," I said. "See you later."

Shanae strode out. It was the last time I saw her alive.

CHAPTER TWO

Assistant State's Attorney Ellen Martinez was nothing, if not completely organized. When I stopped by her office to talk about Tina Jackson, she retrieved the girl's file in an instant—a quick walk to a file cabinet and a glance in one drawer. She wore a white suit. I searched for a spot or stray hair and came up empty. People that neat and organized should be shot.

"Tina Jackson. Let's see." Martinez rocked in her high-backed chair, flipping through the file. She stopped, her eyebrow arched. "First offense. They might have let her slide at intake, if she hadn't broken that poor woman's arm."

"That was an accident," I said. "She never meant to hurt her."

"Little Tina has a mouth on her, too, says here."

"I think her talk is bigger than her walk."

Martinez fixed me with a knowing look. "Really? Well, she's no stranger to the system."

"I thought you said this was her first offense."

"It is. I'm talking about social services." She flipped to another page, placed the file on the desk and tapped a pale pink fingernail on a copy of a court order. "Tina's mother, Shanae Jackson, was ordered into rehab five years ago. She was a crack addict, selling for extra money. None of this might have come out if it hadn't been for the abuse."

"Abuse?"

"A doctor noticed Tina's bruises. It took some doing, but he squeezed the story out of her. Shanae had mood swings. A tendency to fly into rages. One word could set her off. Used to take it out on Tina with an extension cord. One time, she threatened Tina with her own softball bat." Martinez spoke matter-of-factly, like this was the kind of story she'd told many times before. "Clearly, Ms. Jackson had anger management problems, probably aggravated by the crack."

I nodded. Obviously, there was more than the usual mother-daughter friction between Shanae and Tina. "So Tina would have been about eight at the time. Where did social services place her?"

"With the dad, Rodney Fisher. Shanae's brother came down from New York to contest it, but his concerns were dismissed as personal animosity."

"How long did Tina live with Fisher?"

"Close to three years. Shanae was in rehab maybe a year of that time. She filed a petition to regain custody after that. It dragged out, but her brother kept paying the legal bills so . . . ." Martinez's mouth twisted into a look of wry distaste. "The case kept going until Shanae got what she wanted."

I nodded and jotted this information on my notepad. It could be important, not only for Tina's case, but Shanae's request for child support. I wondered if I should feel embarrassed that I hadn't thought to question my own clients on these matters.

Martinez must have read my mind. "I only know this because I've had the file long enough to make some inquiries." She paused and sat up straighter. "And I've been handling juvenile cases long enough to know what inquiries to make."

And you obviously haven't, I mentally finished her statement. "Well, thank you for letting me know," I said, trying to maintain a semblance of poise. "Could I get a copy of your paperwork for my file?"

"Certainly. Happy to help in any way I can."

I reached for the file. "May I take a look?"

She placed it in my hands. "Knock yourself out."

I went through the documentation. Along with what Shanae had given me, I found court filings, DSS forms, and other paperwork related to her rehab, Tina's temporary placement with her father, and the subsequent custody proceeding. I indicated what I wanted copied, and Martinez stepped out with the file a moment to find a secretary to handle it.

"Thanks," I said, upon her return. "So what was your point in bringing all this up?"

"Tina's had it rough. A mostly absent father. A mother with problems of her own." Martinez rounded her desk and sat. "She's reached an age where she's starting to act out. What she does now could mean the difference between staying straight and going off the rails. This first offense could be a warning."

"So what's the bottom line?"

"This *is* her first offense." Martinez toyed with the bent corner of another file, smoothing it with her thumb. "But given the violent nature of the crime and her personal history, I don't want her to get off with a mere slap on the wrist. I'm asking for six months detention, counseling, and restitution for the victim's medical bills."

I stared at her. "Detention? You're kidding, right?"

Martinez shook her head. "I think Tina needs some time in a structured environment. If she's good, they'll probably allow weekend visits with mom."

"Look, I know I haven't handled a lot of juvenile cases, but I've done criminal work. I can think of adults with priors who've pled for better deals than this. What about community service?"

Martinez tucked a stray wisp of dark hair behind her ear and leaned forward. "Juvenile crime is a growing problem in this county," she droned, as if narrating a documentary. "Especially among girls. And this wasn't a minor crime. An elderly woman was hurt. Tina and others like her need to understand there are serious consequences for that." She settled back in her chair and resumed rocking. That simple action irritated me. "Besides," she said. "I think this incident is more than a fluke. I think it's a cry for help."

"Perhaps," I said. "But to lock her up? The punishment seems out of proportion to the crime. Would you settle for fifty hours of community service and court-ordered counseling?"

Martinez crossed her legs, giving me that look of smug assuredness that came from knowing the juvenile master would take her word as gospel and I was just another defense attorney. Scum.

"This isn't negotiable," she said. "If you don't like it, you can always make your pitch to Master Cain."

"You can bet on it," I said. "I trust Cain isn't going to add to the overcrowding at detention centers by locking up a kid on a first offense, just because she's suffered a few hard knocks. Or comes from the wrong neighborhood."

It was Martinez's turn to frown. "This has nothing to do with Tina's neighborhood."

"No, of course not. Or her race either, I'm sure." I leaned forward and Martinez stopped rocking. A minor victory. "Just tell me, when was the last time you sent a white, middle-class kid off to juvie jail for a purse-snatching and a first offense at that? Has it *ever* happened?"

Martinez said nothing. Her assistant came in and handed Martinez the file and the copies. Martinez gave the copies to me.

"I guess that about wraps it up," she said.

She gave me a prim nod and we both rose and shook hands. "Nice to meet you," she said.

Yeah, right, I thought. I felt blindsided by what Martinez had told me, but it was the kind of thing that would have come out sooner or later. Better to learn it now than the hard way later.

What I didn't realize was how many more surprises Tina's case had in store for me.

CHAPTER THREE

I spent a leisurely hour or so in court, watching skittish defendants run through countless guilty plea litanies. Waiting for my client's case to be called gave him plenty of time to learn his lines. He pled to reckless endangerment after being charged with assault. He had drug-related priors too. The assistant state's attorney must have felt generous when we worked out the deal, because he sought only probation before judgment and community service. *When did prosecutors start being so nice?*

Faint anxiety distracted me. I wondered if my erstwhile affair with one of the State's Attorney's most senior prosecutors had leaked out. Could it be that other ASAs were treating me with kid gloves because of that? Didn't seem likely.

My decision to break off the affair with the very-married Ray Mardovich hadn't been easy. And I felt wary whenever I went to court. I'd catch myself looking for Ray and hoping I wouldn't see him (while part of me still hoped I would).

My client went through the guilty plea motions with admirable poise. As I gathered my things and turned to leave, I thought I saw the ASA wink at me as the bailiff called the next case. Could have been my imagination or something in his eye. Paranoid thoughts of my relationship with Ray leaking out plagued me again. If there had been a leak, I hoped the prosecutor wasn't hoping for an encore. Good plea bargains in exchange for good head? What a comforting thought.

If this prosecutor was seeking anything more than professional courtesy, he was wasting his time. My episode with Ray had taught me not to shit where you eat.

As I weaved my way through the courthouse crowd—the usual downtrodden lot in shiny, off-the-rack suits reserved for weddings and funerals—I saw ASA Kaitlyn Farrell approaching, balancing a stack of files. Kait's one of the good ones—always deals fair and square—and a great source of inside information. I flagged her down and drew her aside for some quick face time.

"Sam!" she said. "You're not here to see me, are you?"

"Naw. Nothing in your league. A juvenile matter and an assault." Kait's forte was major weapons charges. In Prince George's County, enough gun and drug cases rolled through the system to support a whole unit. "But I'm heading out to meet Walt Shapiro on an interesting case."

Her eyes widened behind the black rectangular frames that complemented her dark brown hair. "Do tell. What kind of case are you handling with the Grand Master of PG County criminal lawyers? Anything where I might be on the other side?"

"Doubtful. It's an embezzlement case."

"White collar crime? My, my—we're moving up in the world, aren't we?" She pushed her glasses up the bridge of her nose. "Even Walt doesn't do a whole lot of those."

"Consider the market. Most of the criminal work around here is in drugs and violent crime." PG County had a drug trafficking and murder rate to rival its neighbor, Washington, DC. "I think Walt stumbled onto this one because it involves his nephew, Bradley Higgins."

"Really? What's he like?"

"All right, I guess. One of these young guys who's into computer games, so he works for a computer gaming company. He works in accounting, has big ideas about going into business for himself someday. He's okay, if you go for boyish blonds with too much family money and too little sense."

Kait laughed, then looked thoughtful. "Embezzlement . . . not my bailiwick. But don't kid yourself. Our Economic Crimes Unit has plenty of cases. Mortgage fraud is rampant in this county. I'm not sure which of their attorneys would handle embezzlement, though."

"Hold your horses. The company hasn't even pressed charges yet. All they have on him is a phony vendor account they claim he created in order to steal from the company. Since he's the only one authorized to create these accounts, naturally, he came under suspicion first."

"Sounds logical."

"Yes, but . . . " I held up a finger for emphasis, "he was the one who reported the irregularity that led to the investigation of the account."

"So why would they suspect him?"

"He reported it to his former supervisor but never put anything in writing. He thinks the supervisor took credit for finding the problem, since it was his job to spot these things. Anyway, the supervisor quit or was fired—it's not clear which—and no one knows where he's gone. Or at least no one's telling."

"So all you have is his word about reporting the problem. And he could be lying to the company and you."

"Anything's possible," I said. "But I believe him. Besides, if the case against him is so clear cut, why didn't they fire him instead of putting him on administrative leave pending an audit? Obviously, they need more evidence before they can take legal action."

I'd left out a few details. Sure, Brad's old supervisor, a fellow named Darrell Cooper, could have taken credit for finding the phony account. Cooper, perhaps too conveniently, wasn't around to confirm or deny it. The corporate headquarters had quickly sent a woman named Sondra Jones to take Cooper's place. And what about the $5,000 they found hidden in Brad's file cabinet? Not a smart place to hide stolen money, but who said criminals were always smart?

Kait shifted the files to her other arm. "Sounds like a live one. But wait'll you hear this!" She leaned in with a conspiratorial air. "Mardovich and his wife have split."

My jaw dropped. For a moment, I couldn't think of a word to say. "Really?" I murmured.

Kait nodded, looking coy. "You know why, don't you?"

I felt my heart skip a beat and feared I might break out in a sweat. *Please don't tell me Helen found out about us. And the whole State's Attorney's Office knows.*

Kait smiled. "You remember Amy Hinson, right? Or was she after your time?"

It took me a few seconds to absorb her words. "Amy Hinson," I repeated. "The paralegal?" *Amy.*

"Right. Tell me you're not surprised?" She shot me a knowing look over her glasses. "She's young, she's cute, and she's smart. And she's been assisting him on a lot of cases."

"Of course."

"They've been seeing each other for over a year."

My mouth opened, but I couldn't speak. I'd only broken up with Ray a few months ago.

Kaitlyn nodded. "Got it straight from Amy. Technically, she's young enough to be his daughter. I mean if he, like, had a kid in high school."

"Over a year, huh?"

"Says Amy."

"Well . . . ." I couldn't think of a thing to add. My cheeks burned.

"I'd love to chat more, but I gotta scoot and get ready for the mid-morning docket. Good luck," she called over her shoulder, as she plunged back into the throng.

I forced a smile and waved, but my mind was reeling with the thoughts of Ray's incredible duplicity. Fearing that I might confront him—or kill him, I stomped out of the courthouse. Staying couldn't lead anywhere good.

φφφ

I left Upper Marlboro and took back roads, foot heavy on the pedal, to get to Walt's office in Greenbelt. My plan was to run by Kozmik Games, the computer gaming company Brad worked for, and check his computer. Perhaps I'd find support for his claims of innocence. Since Brad's office was right down the road from Walt's, I decided to stop at Walt's office first. What I had to say was better discussed in person. Besides, seeing Walt might take my mind off the news about that fucking jerk, Ray.

It was a sunny October day, and I had the top down on my purple '67 Mustang so I could savor the last of the mild weather before November's chill moved in. I glanced around at the unobstructed view of trees, their yellow and orange leaves splashed across a royal blue sky. The day's beauty seemed to mock me. *Damn Ray!* I refused to fall apart and pushed aside my anger, hurt, and jealousy for the time being.

I made my way to Kenilworth Avenue, proceeding to where it narrows abruptly from six-lane highway to two-lane country road. I turned left onto a street flanked by office parks. Another turn and I pulled into the lot. The place was a three-minute drive from the Greenbelt Metro station and a stone's throw from the federal courthouse, a gleaming granite and glass building. Though a decade had passed, Walt still called it the "new" federal courthouse. For him, the

Maryland federal district court would always be the one up in Baltimore.

I parked outside the building where Walt rented his small, top-floor suite. After bestowing an admiring glance on the "Darth Vader buildings" across the street—two matching mid-rise cubes of bluish-black glass—I headed inside.

A quick elevator ride later, I strolled through reception, past the empty desk and the glassed-in conference room, to Walt's office. I could hear him talking. His door was open, so I wandered in. He gave me a quick wave and gestured to a leather chair while he continued his phone conversation. I pointed toward the kitchen and mouthed, "Coffee," and he nodded. I took my time. Knowing Walt's phone habits, there was no need to rush.

During those few minutes while I waited for him, I did some deep breathing exercises. In. Out. In. Out. I visualized punching Ray in the face (or better yet, kicking him in the balls). Keep breathing, I told myself. In. Out. In. Out. I kept it up until I nearly hyperventilated.

I retrieved a ceramic beer stein from the cabinet and filled it up. After a few minutes, I heard Walt say, "All right. Great talking to you. Bye!" The phone clicked into its cradle, and Walt groaned. "Man, I need more coffee. Sorry to keep you waiting. I haven't spoken to Jake in a coon's age." He wandered into the kitchen with his favorite mug—*Illegitimi Non Carborundum* imprinted on it—in one hand, a file in the other. He set the mug on the counter and poured coffee to the rim.

"No biggie," I said. Based on Walt's track record, the wait had amounted to a millisecond. "I see Laverne is off today."

"That girl! Always sick. She's lucky I keep her on." Walt's eyes were gleaming slits on each side of his slightly bulbous nose. A smile stretched across his rubbery face. "Laverne" was his nonexistent receptionist. The reception desk was a prop, for the most part, except when Walt hired a temp. Otherwise, "Laverne" was the butt of our running jokes about her taking too much leave or too many trips to the bathroom.

"So," he said. "To what do I owe the pleasure of your company?"

"I was in the neighborhood on my way to Kozmik and hoped to get a few minutes of your time. I want to talk about Brad's case."

"Really?" He glanced at his watch. "Brad'll be here in a few minutes if you want to talk to him, too. We're having lunch."

"Actually, I just wanted to talk to you." Trying to appear casual, I took a long sip of coffee and considered my next words carefully. "You're pretty fond of Brad, aren't you?"

"Fond? He's the closest thing I have to a son." He averted his eyes before adding, "At least, now . . . ."

I felt a flush of shame for bringing it up. Walt's divorce was decades ago. It had been so bitter, his own son had refused to speak to him since. I'd never asked the details. It was ancient history and none of my business.

"Let me be blunt. Do you think it's possible that he's lying to us?"

His eyebrows gnarled in concern. "Hell, it's possible that all our clients are lying to us," he said, in a tone that suggested the obviousness of that proposition. He glanced sidelong at me as he sipped his coffee. "Why?" he asked.

"Well, I was just thinking, Brad does have a bit of a history."

Walt shot me a look. "That's putting it rather delicately, isn't it?"

"I can be less delicate, if you prefer. He's had legal problems before."

"Frat house high jinks." He pulled a sour face. "Frankly, I think my sister spoiled the boy." He shook his finger at me. "But I don't think Brad's a criminal."

"When we spoke, he struck me as defensive and a bit argumentative."

25

Walt waved a hand. "The boy was just nervous and tired of answering questions."

"Sure," I said. I wasn't buying it. "We'd better hope the audit clears him. If Kozmik presses charges, Brad won't respond well to a cop's third degree. He could barely stand the first degree."

"I know, I know." Walt held up a placating hand. "When someone checks the computer system there, I hope it shows that a hacker created that account."

"Yes," I said. "I hope so. I also hope the company agrees to do it, and whatever they find clears Brad. I intend to run a background check on Brad when I do one on his old boss, Darrell Cooper, and the guy who previously held Brad's job. Vince whats-his-name."

"Vince Marzetti."

"Right. You would do that with any other client."

I turned from Walt. Brad stood at the kitchen door. Tall and hunched the way tall people often are, he was in his mid-twenties. He had a boyish face with soft, delicate features, and sandy-blond hair. Brad's glance drifted my way, his gray eyes guarded and his mouth set in a sullen line. I wondered how much he'd heard of our conversation.

"Hi, Uncle Walt," he said.

"Brad, my boy!" Brad managed a slight smile as Walt turned to greet him, setting his cup down to shake Brad's hand and give him a one-armed embrace. "You remember Sam?"

Brad nodded. He looked about as enthused as he had at our initial meeting. "Hi," he said.

"I should be going," I said, delaying a moment to wash my mug.

A look of relief washed across Walt's features. "Good luck with your visit. I assume you'll be talking to your friend while you're there?"

"Friend?" I drew a blank then recovered. "You mean their general counsel, Leonard Hirschbeck?" I snorted. "I know the man, but we're hardly friends."

I finished rinsing my mug and placed it on the drying rack. "Take it easy, Walt. Nice to see you again Brad."

Brad grunted. I guess I'd left him speechless with awe.

CHAPTER FOUR

I left Walt's. The mention of Leonard Hirschbeck had taken my mind off Ray and onto Brad Higgins's problems. Kozmik Games was a short trip down Kenilworth Avenue to a small outcropping of mid-rise office buildings just past Greenbelt Park—an anomalous national park and camping area amid suburban development. The buildings had a slightly worn air, like the post-WWII single-family homes in the neighborhood. The small brick houses, once the stronghold of white, working-class folk, had changed hands over the past thirty years to include a broader cross-section of ethnicities.

Kozmik had offices on the third and fourth floors. I took the elevator to four where the company logo covered the opposite wall—"Kozmik Games" in cartoonish yellow letters against a blue oval background dotted with small yellow stars and planets. The hallway ran almost the length of the building, ending in perpendicular hallways on each side, like a big capital "I." Turning left, I headed toward the accounting offices.

I stepped inside a large room and strolled to the end of an aisle bisecting rows of bland gray cubicles. To my right were two private offices, their doors closed. A Led Zeppelin poster caught my eye.

The room was hushed but for the clicking of keyboards.

I peered into the first cube, where a lanky fellow was entering numbers onto a spreadsheet. I stole past him and proceeded to the workspace at the far end. A nameplate on the divider read "Bradley Higgins."

Brad had an L-shaped desk tucked into the cubicle. His chair faced away from the entrance, providing visitors a stellar view of his back. I recalled the story of Wild Bill Hickok, shot from behind while playing poker with his back to the door. A file cabinet obscured my view of the monitor. From this vantage point, no mortal could have read the code Brad used to create the account.

I crossed to the desk and sat down. Craning my head, I examined the ceiling and its juncture with the wall behind me. No evidence of a security camera. Too bad. It might have revealed the identity of whoever planted the money. Of course, someone in the company would have gained that information too.

I turned on Brad's computer. It beeped, and the monitor sprang to life with a soft click and a hiss. A message on a blue screen asked me to enter my user name and password. I put in the information Brad had given me and got an error message. Damn! Someone had changed it. Of course. I felt frustrated that I couldn't double check his email messages for evidence to support what he'd told us.

"Can I help you?" The lanky fellow peered at me.

I got up and extended my hand. "I'm Sam McRae. I'm a lawyer, representing Brad Higgins."

"Jon Fielding." He gave my hand a half-hearted squeeze. His gaze drifted to a spot over my shoulder, then returned to me. "Technically," he said, lowering his voice. "I'm not supposed to talk to anyone about Brad."

"Then I won't ask about him. Can you tell me if this office has security cameras in it?"

Fielding shook his head. "Not that I know of. Why?"

"Just curious." It was possible there were cameras the employees didn't know about and possible they'd recorded something the company hadn't told us about. Possibilities I'd have to explore with Hirschbeck.

Fielding looked over my shoulder again. "I don't think you should be on his computer, either."

"I'm sorry," I said, keeping my voice low to match his. "I can't get in anyway."

I stole a glance back at the monitor and noticed the screen saver had already kicked in. A multicolored, amorphous shape undulated against a black background. Looking at that for ten minutes would have driven me mad.

"I just wanted to check for anything that would support his story," I told Fielding. "Nothing cloak-and-dagger."

"Well, if you need a character witness for him, I'll be one." He glanced around.

"You don't believe he did it?"

"I don't believe it, no." He paused and looked down. "I . . . can't really say more."

"That's all right. I don't want you to get into trouble over this."

"Excuse me, ma'am." A female voice piped up behind Fielding. It belonged to a short woman, her dark eyes fixing me with a stare both curious and hostile. She had a round face, olive complexion and short dark-brown hair, shellacked into a spiky punk do. A faux ruby nose ring gleamed under the fluorescents.

"Who are you?" she asked.

I introduced myself again and explained why I was there.

"You shouldn't be here." She flashed a look at Fielding. I didn't catch his reaction, but her full lips pursed in a way that told me she didn't like it. "We've been instructed by our general counsel not to talk about this with anyone. You should take any questions to him. His name is Leonard Hirschbeck."

"I know who he is. And you are?"

"Ana Lopez. I've taken Brad's position."

"You're filling in for Brad," Fielding said. "Temporarily."

"Yeah? We'll see how temporary it is." She crossed her arms and stared me down once more. "I think you should leave now."

"Ana, lighten up," Fielding said.

"Don't tell me to lighten up! I'm doing what I've been told. And you'd do the same, in my place. Not that you'd know anything about that."

Heads poked up over the cubicle tops and disappeared quickly. It reminded me of Whack-A-Mole.

"You seem pretty convinced of his guilt," I said.

"Well, look at the facts. The account was set up a month after Brad started. Only he had control over its creation and maintenance. Then they found all that money in his file cabinet. Coincidence?"

"If they thought Brad was guilty, why didn't they fire him?" I asked.

Ana re-pursed her lips and said, "You need to speak to Mr. Hirschbeck." Her look told me that any further inquiry would be at my own risk.

"Okay, okay," I said, raising my hands. "I'm outta here." I glanced at Fielding, whose lips curled in a grimace. He shrugged and gave me a *what can I do?* look.

I left the room, but waited outside the door. There was a brief back-and-forth I couldn't make out between Fielding and Lopez, then silence. When I was pretty sure the coast was clear, I snuck back in and handed Fielding one of my cards.

"Call me," I mouthed. He nodded and stuck the card in his shirt pocket.

I scampered out, knowing where two employees on the accounting staff stood.

At the opposite end of the long hall was Big Wig Central, where Brad said the president had his corner office and his veeps huddled around him for warmth. I could put my tail between my legs and slink off or I could try talking to Sondra Jones in Cooper's stead. So talk to her, I thought. What's the worst that could happen? She'll tell me to leave her alone and talk to Hirschbeck. Or not. Nothing ventured, nothing gained.

I walked into an anteroom large enough for ten desks. I counted four. One, with a monitor and a phone that resembled the console of the Starship Enterprise, faced the door. The rest were perpendicular to the wall and near three office doors. A long black vinyl sofa with gleaming chrome legs filled the opposite wall. Magazines covered a faux-wood coffee table. Freestanding cabinets and shelving completed the decor.

At a far desk, a twenty-something woman with carrot-colored hair and a black micro-miniskirt chatted with a light-skinned black woman.

"Could you believe when he shot her? I couldn't believe that," the black woman said.

"Yeah, that shocked the hell out of me."

I hoped they were talking about a movie or a TV show. I looked around, saw Sondra Jones's name on a door and headed for it.

From the corner of my eye, I noticed the black woman gesture my way. Red rushed over to intercept me, tugging at the skirt hem which barely concealed her underwear preference. "Can I help you?"

"I'm here to see Sondra Jones," I said, attempting an authoritative voice.

"Do you have an appointment?" Red went to the front desk and checked a calendar.

"No. But this is very important. I'm investigating the situation involving Bradley Higgins." Okay, I'd left a few details out, but I wasn't lying.

Her eyes widened. "Then she'll want to talk to you. Can I have your name, please?"

"Sam McRae."

"One moment." She picked up the phone and I heard a faint ring coming from Jones's office. She relayed the information to Jones then put her hand over the phone. "Are you with the police?" I shook my head. She told Jones, said "Okay," then hung up.

"She'll be out in just a moment," she said, in a solemn voice.

"Thanks." While inspecting a poster of an old pinball game over the sofa, I heard the door open and turned to see one of the tallest, thinnest women I'd ever laid eyes on. She wore a black suit and a pair of black spike-heeled pumps. Her raven hair, cut in an expensive careless shag, framed a pale face, pointed chin, cat-like green eyes and bright red lips.

"Come in and have a seat, Ms. McRae," she said, with a lightness in her tone that contrasted with her appearance. She followed me into the office and closed the door before shaking my hand. "Sondra Jones. Since you're not with the police, may I assume you're a private investigator?"

"No. Actually, I'm an attorney representing Bradley Higgins."

"I see." She stiffened slightly. "Just a moment." She picked up her phone and punched four buttons. "Len," she said. "There's a lawyer here about the Higgins matter. I need you to come to my office. Now." So much for catching her off-guard.

"Our general counsel is coming," she said, as she hung up. "He insists on being present at any meetings we have with lawyers."

"I understand. While we're waiting, I was wondering if your offices have hidden security cameras."

Jones kept silent.

"Seen any good movies lately?" I asked.

Jones simply folded her hands. It appeared that even the most mundane chatter had to be monitored by Hirschbeck now. The silence stretched into an interminable five minutes before someone knocked.

The door opened and Leonard Hirschbeck came in. He was only a couple of inches taller than my own five foot eight. He'd put on weight since I'd dated him in law school, and his curly brown hair was receding. From the look on his face, I knew he was as happy to see me as I was to see him.

Jones and I got up. "This is Leonard Hirschbeck, general counsel for Kozmik Games. Len, this is—"

"Sam McRae," he said.

Jones's cat eyes registered surprise. "You've met?"

"It's been a while," I said. *But not nearly long enough.* "I'm here to talk about Bradley Higgins."

"I thought Walt Shapiro was his attorney."

"I'm assisting Walt."

"How nice for you. Did you make an appointment?"

"No, I was in the neighborhood—" Again, it was the truth.

"Sure you were. You have nerve, you know, coming in here and questioning a company employee without going through me."

"I wasn't aware I needed your permission."

"Maybe you should reread the Code of Ethics. You can get in trouble for contacting clients who have legal counsel. Surely you know that."

Bullshit. And who are you *to be preaching about ethics?*

"Now, Len, you know that rule applies only to cases in litigation," I said, with syrupy politeness. "And, with all due respect, I had no idea Ms. Jones was authorized to speak for the company. That's part of the rule, too, you know."

Hirschbeck's eyes narrowed.

"You didn't know?" I gaped in mock surprise. "Maybe *you* should reread the Code of Ethics."

"What the hell do you want?"

"I was just asking Ms. Jones about the security system in your offices. I'm wondering if you have security cameras set up. If so, they might reveal the person who placed the money in Brad's file cabinet."

"If we did, you can be sure we would have thought to check them by now."

"So, yes or no. Do you have them?"

"No, we do not. No hidden cameras. No secret microphones." He rolled his eyes.

"Then why did you decide to search his cubicle?"

"Our employees don't have a complete expectation of privacy in their work areas. We can search them whenever we want, for whatever reason. You should know that." Hirschbeck snarled. "This is a private business. When it comes to employee matters, we have a lot of latitude— including searching offices, desks, and what-have-you. And firing people."

"Brad claims he actually raised concerns with his former boss about the phony vendor account. Do you have anything to prove otherwise?"

Jones started to open her mouth, but Hirschbeck cut in, like a trial lawyer registering an objection before the witness could answer. "We'll have an independent auditor conduct a full investigation of this matter, but our decision to search Mr. Higgins's cubicle was based on reasonable conclusions drawn from the evidence we had at the time."

"What about his boss, Darrell Cooper? Why did you fire him?"

"Who says we did?"

"Well, he left rather quickly. Did you fire him?"

"I'm not going to comment on that."

"Did he leave on his own?"

"No comment. That has nothing to do with your client's situation."

"How do you know that? In fact, if Cooper was responsible for overseeing these accounts, why aren't you investigating him, too?"

Hirschbeck glowered at me. "As I said, we are in the process of hiring an independent auditor. When the audit is complete, we will be happy to share the results, to the extent they are not otherwise privileged."

I felt sure that Hirschbeck would be very busy coming up with privileges to assert. "I'm assuming that you'll also have a computer forensics expert make sure no one hacked into the accounts payable system."

Hirschbeck looked at me as if I was speaking in tongues. "You must be joking."

"Not at all," I said. "It's possible someone did just that."

"And we have to cough up the money for an expert, based on a mere possibility? I think not. It's not up to us to prove our system *hasn't* been tampered with."

"Cooper worked in accounting. Perhaps he found a way to do it."

"I told you, I have nothing further to say about him."

"Is there some reason why you're so reluctant to discuss Cooper—and why he left? Or the reasons you decided to search Brad's workspace?" I leaned in for emphasis. "Is it because you have so very little?"

His face reddened. "We have more than you know," he blustered. "A certain individual has shared information—on a confidential basis. The person prefers to remain anonymous, due to fear of retaliation by your client."

So someone spoke out against Brad. I had to wonder if it was Attitudinal Ana. "Brad Higgins wouldn't hurt a fly. And he has the right to confront his accusers. I'd like to talk to this person. You can be there, if you wish. Just an informal discussion. Off the record." Not that there was any record to be on, at this point.

"I'm afraid that won't be possible." Hirschbeck bared his teeth in a fake smile. "Suffice it to say, we are confident that our actions, so far, are legally justifiable."

"It won't suffice at all. For all I know, you have nothing. Your source may be biased. Maybe has an ax to grind. Or something to hide. My client says he's innocent. You've placed him under a microscope and put his livelihood and career at risk. It had better be based on more than accusations by an anonymous witness and evidence planted in his office."

"Planted?" Hirschbeck turned beet red. "I'll sue you for slander."

"I didn't say *you* did it. Is there a reason for you to take that remark so personally?"

We faced each other down, like gunfighters. I averted my eyes and glanced at Jones, to keep from laughing out loud at Hirschbeck's mask of righteous indignation. Jones stood there, blinking, her gaze flitting back and forth between us.

The phone rang. Jones picked it up. "Yes," she said, in a dull voice. "Okay." When she hung up, she said, "My three-thirty is here."

"That's all right," Hirschbeck said. His vocal chords sounded tight as bridge cables. "Ms. McRae was just leaving."

I turned to Jones. "It was nice meeting you," I said. "Maybe sometime we'll be allowed to have an actual conversation." I walked out with as much dignity as I could muster. Hirschbeck trailed behind. The two women sat hunched over their desks in the anteroom, making a show of not watching us leave. Jones's "three-thirty," some guy dressed like an insurance salesman, was too engrossed in reading outdated celebrity news to spare us a glance.

Hirschbeck followed me to the elevator. I wanted to tell him to fuck off. "It would make everything a lot easier if we cooperated with each other," I said.

"You'll get what you're due in time," he growled.

"Len-ny," I said, in a mock pleading tone. He hated being called that. "Why are you doing this? Is it really to protect a confidential source? Or are you still angry, after all these years, that I broke it off with you?"

The elevator arrived. I got on, half expecting Hirschbeck to follow. Instead he snorted, "Don't flatter yourself. You're not that hot."

"In that case, I can't wait to learn what you're hiding," I shot back as the doors closed.

CHAPTER FIVE

I rushed back to my office for a late meeting with a little old lady who wanted a will done. Before she arrived, I phoned Reed Duvall, a private eye I'd befriended while working opposite sides of a recent case.

"Got some work for you," I said.

"And I've got a problem with you."

"Don't worry," I said. "I'm not looking for a handout. This is paying business I'm offering." Duvall knew I usually did my own case research and investigation, since most of my clients couldn't afford him.

"That's my problem," Duvall chided me. "All you ever call me about is business."

I blushed and felt slightly heady. Thoughts of Ray brought me down to earth with a thud. *The last thing you need is to get involved with someone else you work with.* Duvall wasn't married, but still . . . what if it didn't work out? I didn't want to ruin a perfectly good friendship. So I ignored his comment.

Affecting a breezy voice, I said, "You'll be happy to know, this is for a case I'm handling with Walt Shapiro. I've got his blessing and budget to back me."

I gave him a thumbnail sketch of the situation with Brad Higgins and asked for a background check on him, Darrell Cooper and Vince Marzetti. I wanted to know if any of them had made huge bank deposits or bought high-ticket items recently. I also asked him to track down the missing Darrell Cooper and see what he could find on ITN Consultants.

"When did Cooper quit?" Duvall asked.

"Week and a half ago."

"If he's moved, his new address won't show up in any databases for at least a couple of months. You need this information sooner than that, I guess."

"The sooner, the better. This guy may have ripped off the company and left our client twisting in the wind."

"I'll come up with something. I'm sure there's a creative way to get at this."

We both knew I didn't want to hear what that was. "Thanks, Duvall. I'd have a go at finding him myself, but no one wants to talk to a lawyer. Plus, I'd be violating ethical rules if I pretended to be anything else."

"If you can't figure out a way around those rules, you must not be doing your job." I heard suppressed laughter.

"Ha ha. Anyhow, you're my way around the rules."

"Thank God for dirty work. Keeps me in business."

"Keeps us all in business. Makes the world go 'round."

"Do I detect a note of cynicism?"

I sighed. "Cynicism? Or resignation that we're all swimming in the same cesspool?"

"Listen to you. You need a vacation."

A vacation. The concept seemed as bizarre as a pole dancer at a ballroom competition. When was the last time I'd *had* a real vacation? There was the two weeks I'd taken off before leaving the PD's office. I did the math. Four years? Had it really been four years? With the workload building and the new case with Walt—it didn't look like I'd be vacationing again any time soon.

His voice interrupted my mental pity party. "I'll have something for you by tomorrow. After that, I'm out of town for a week."

"Business or pleasure?"

"Family business down in North Carolina. Talk to you soon. And cheer up, okay?"

We hung up. I pondered my gloomy mood. The day's irritations left me feeling sour and out of sorts.

When I got to the office the following morning, I had a voice mail message from Jon Fielding at Kozmik Games. I returned the call, only to have him insist on calling me back in ten minutes. I used the time to bang out a demand letter I'd been meaning to write for days. The slip-and-fall case involved a dancer named Daria Lewellin who thought she could claim her bruised knee as a career-ending disability and settle for millions. Not gonna happen, I thought as I requested a dollar amount with as many zeros as I could muster without laughing out loud.

The phone rang as I printed the letter.

"Sorry," Fielding said. "I had to find a private place to talk. I don't want Ana or anyone else listening in."

"What's the big secret?"

"I don't know. I just know this Brad situation has made everyone paranoid." Fielding spoke in a low, clipped voice. I could visualize his eyes darting around. "We've been ordered not to discuss Brad or the embezzlement with anyone. People here are even afraid to talk about it with each other."

"Why?"

"I can't talk much longer." His words came out in a rush. "Just ask Vince Marzetti. I think he knew about that account before he left the company."

"So you're saying the account existed before Brad began working there?"

"I think so. Ask Vince. He'll know." The line went dead.

I went through my mail, searching for answers to interrogatories I'd sent weeks ago in a messy, slow-moving

Debbi Mack

divorce—one of those cases you regret taking the moment you find out who the other attorney is. Steve Woodrow, aka "Slippery Steve," was living down to his reputation. I'd called Steve several times about the answers he owed, only to end up in voice mail. He had never returned my calls. I dialed, got his voice mail again, and left another message. It took all my self-control not to pepper the message with expletives.

I didn't see a cashier's check or money order from Shanae Jackson for her child support case. No tickee, no laundry. It was Thursday— only two days since we'd met. I'd give her until Monday. After that, we'd have to talk. Maybe her brother wasn't as obliging about paying my retainer as she'd expected.

I was wrapping up for the day when the phone rang. Could it be Slippery Steve returning a message? Dream on, I thought, picking up the phone.

"Ms. McRae?" The voice was deep and unfamiliar. "My name is William Jackson. I'm Shanae Jackson's brother."

"What can I do for you, Mr. Jackson?" I steeled myself to give a polite, but firm, "no" to any hard-luck story.

"My sister . . . " His voice broke. "My sister is dead."

I was too stunned to speak. "D-d-dead? What happened?"

"She was murdered. Someone beat her to death with a softball bat las' night." His words slurred. I wondered if he'd been drinking. "A neighbor found her this mornin'. Her back door was open and she jus' walked in and found her on the kitchen floor." He took a deep breath and sighed. "I drove down here from New York right after I heard."

"Oh, my God. I'm so sorry. Was it a break-in?"

"I don't know. Cops didn't tell me nuthin'. They did say they couldn't find a purse or identification. The neighbor knew her from her clothes and a cross she wore on a chain. Her face . . . " Again, his voice cut off. I could hear the pain in it—and in his silence. "Her face was smashed in. I could barely recognize her myself," he sobbed.

44

I took a moment to absorb the horror of the situation. How would Tina deal with her mother's murder? If Shanae had been found that morning, she must have been killed sometime after Tina left for school. I hoped the police had contacted Tina's school or her father before the girl came home.

"I'm so sorry for your loss, Mr. Jackson. Is Tina all right? Where will she stay?" Concern aside, I needed to note the change of address in her file.

"She supposed to stay with her father. So, she's all right—kinda."

"What does that mean?"

"It means the man may say she's stayin' there, but half the time, she ain't gonna be there."

"Where else would she be?"

"Who knows? She might stay with friends, but that don't mean much. I don't know these friends. I don't know how far to trust 'em." He paused. I could hear his labored breathing. "I think Tina's fallen in with a bad crowd, Ms. McRae. I told Shanae it was just a matter of time before she got into trouble. And Rodney ain't gonna lif' a finger to stop her."

"Hold it, hold it." I tried to stem the flow of his words with a question. "Why do you think he's the one to blame for Tina's behavior?"

"Tina's problems started after Shanae went into the drug program, you know. When she was livin' with Rodney."

I thought about that. "According to someone familiar with Shanae's history, she was abusing Tina. That in itself could have contributed—"

"I'm telling you it started with Rodney!" He wasn't going to hear otherwise, regardless of the facts. "I told Shanae, what with her working two jobs, taking care of Tina was too much for her. I even offered to take the child in with me, cause she knows her Uncle Bill won't take any of her grief.

But Shanae wouldn't hear it. Maybe she weren't much of a mother, but she loved that girl."

I took notes for my file, the cynic in me wondering if Shanae held onto Tina for love or money. Fisher had paid some child support, even if it wasn't all that he owed. Shanae had been getting some financial benefit from having custody of Tina. She might not have wanted to give it up.

"So what's her dad's number? In case I need to reach Tina."

He gave me Fisher's home and work phone. "But you'd be better off calling her cell phone," he added.

I hadn't thought to get her cell phone number when we met. I forgot that every kid has one. Uncle Bill gave me the number.

"If Tina listens to you," I said, "you should encourage her to stay home and out of trouble." *At least, until we get her current situation resolved,* my inner cynic interjected.

"I'll do what I can. And now I need you to do something for me."

"What's that?"

"I want to be Tina's guardian. I want you to handle it."

"How does her father feel about this?" I had a funny feeling that the father was clueless.

"Father?" Jackson bellowed. "Since when has that man been a father? Was he there for her when she was sick? When she needed advice? Did he give her gifts at Christmas? Or even a birthday card?" Jackson continued to recite a laundry list of Rodney Fisher's various malfeasances. His speech was rushed, his words garbled. He paused to catch his breath. "What has the man done, 'cept not be there for her?"

"He took her in when her mother was in rehab. And he is her father. Unless he's willing to give up his parental rights, to become Tina's guardian, you'll have to show that he's unfit."

He grumbled. "He's unfit, all right. I tole' that court not to let him have her. And what happened? She grew up wild, that's what. He never gave her no ground rules, no guidance. How fit a parent can a man like that be?"

It seemed to me Shanae had fallen short in that regard, too. Now was not the time to bring it up. William Jackson had already made up his mind.

"Have you spoken to Tina's father about this?"

"Yes, I've spoken to him." His voice grew stronger. "And the son of a bitch told me to go to hell."

"Bad news, Mr. Jackson. The burden is on you to prove he's an unfit parent."

"Well, how hard could that be? With Tina running wild every night and him not lifting a finger to stop her."

"You might be able to prove it. Trying to do it now might hurt Tina's defense in the purse-snatching incident. I intend to emphasize the good things about Tina. I need to steer clear of the issue of her 'bad friends,' if at all possible."

He was silent a moment. "What does that mean?"

"It means the cases present a conflict of interest. One I'm not sure I can work around."

"I see." Except for his breathing, he fell silent. "Then I suppose that ends our business."

"It would help me a lot if we could keep in touch. I'm concerned about Tina's welfare. If what you're saying is true—"

"Thank you, anyway, Ms. McRae."

"I'm sorry I couldn't be more help to you. I appreciate . . . Hello?"

Uncle Bill had already hung up.

φφφ

I left a message for Tina to call me. After I hung up, I thought about Ellen Martinez's comment about Tina going "off the rails." Maybe she was. Maybe being raised by an angry, overworked mother had spurred her to deviant behavior. With her mother dead, Tina was left with a poor excuse for a father who allegedly forgot her birthdays.

I strained to remember what it was like to be 13. When I entered my teen years, my parents had been four years dead. Although my life with them in Bed-Stuy had been far from idyllic, loneliness overcame me, as I recalled the void left by their deaths. I shivered and redirected my thoughts elsewhere.

The memory of my cousin took its place, Addie stepping in like a *deus ex machina* and whisking me off to live with her in Takoma Park, Maryland, saving me from the tender mercies of life in a New York City foster home. Not that Addie was perfect. Her idea of cooking was adding hot water to Ramen noodles or heating a frozen pizza. And her financial situation was precarious at best. Yet for reasons known only to her, she'd taken charge of me when other relatives hadn't bothered.

One of the biggest mysteries of my life concerned my grandparents. Why had they cut and run after my parents died? How come they hadn't stepped up and taken me in?

I recall asking Addie. She simply laughed and said, "Your grandparents are assholes. You want to live with assholes?"

I hadn't wanted to live with them. I'd never met them, but would have appreciated their occasional attention. I never came to terms with their behavior, why they never bothered to get know me.

Again, I wrested my attention from the memory. It didn't matter now. None of it mattered. I had learned how to fend for myself thanks to their negligence. Tina, on the other hand . . . .

Would juvenile detention help Tina? Would community service or talking to a counselor make a difference? Maybe. One thing I did know: I would fight to get Tina the best deal possible. If I could only figure out what that was.

CHAPTER SIX

By the next day, Duvall had run the background checks and found nothing suspicious. Since the records could be out of date, he said he'd recheck them periodically. He found addresses for Darrell Cooper in Philadelphia and Vince Marzetti in Frederick, a historic Maryland town 50 miles north of Washington, D.C. He found no record of ITN Consultants. What a surprise.

Again, I tried to reach Tina Jackson and was sent to her voice mail. I left a third message and, uncharacteristically, my cell number. *Leave a client my cell number? They must be wearing parkas in Hell.*

My next call was to Tina's guidance counselor at Silver Hill Intermediate School. "Good morning, Frank Powell speaking." He had the velvet voice of a deejay.

"Mr. Powell, this is Sam McRae. I'm an attorney representing Tina Jackson, one of your students. I understand you're her guidance counselor."

"I am. What can I do for you, Ms. McRae?"

"Well, for starters, you can call me Sam. Tina's run into a bit of legal trouble. I'm hoping to get some background information about her academics, her home life, and her disciplinary record, among other things. I want to confirm a few things she told me." And, maybe, find out what she didn't.

"All right, Sam. I'll need to run by admin to pick up the disciplinary records, but that's not a problem. Call me Frank, by the way. I assume you have a signed release from one of her parents?"

"Yes, I do." Shanae had signed the release the last time she was in my office. The only time. Before she was bludgeoned to death. "Would it be convenient for us to meet sometime today, Frank?"

"I have some meetings this morning, but my afternoon's open, if you want to drop by." His deejay voice made the invitation sound like an ad for a tire sale.

"I'll be there around 1:30 or so."

φφφ

I stopped home for a quick sandwich before heading to the school in Suitland, an inside-the-Beltway D.C. suburb that had seen better days—long before my time. Near the District line, P.G. County is mostly black, mostly poor, and mostly avoided by those who don't fit that mold. The housing ran to old brick structures squeezed onto tiny lots with scrubby lawns and mid-rise apartment buildings—brick boxes whose windows provided joyless views of cracked macadam lots filled with hoopties of every description, from beat-up compacts to classic pimpmobiles.

I parked in the school lot. My purple '67 Mustang, out of place with my peers' gleaming Beemers and Porsches, blended well with the staff's economy cars. Feeling a rush of solidarity with hard-working civil servants, I sauntered into the building.

A security guard escorted me to the main office, where I signed in and got a visitor's pass. We wove through throngs of uniformed students. Loud voices and laughter echoed off the metal lockers.

At once, I felt conspicuous—a strange white woman in a suit, the lone white face in the crowd. I flashed back to my childhood in Bed-Stuy. At six years old on my first day at school, I was the only white kid in my class. It provided an excellent training ground for years of not fitting in.

I shook off the déjà vu, keeping my head high and moving with purpose and confidence, like I belonged there. The way I'd learned in Brooklyn.

The guidance department was a short walk down the hall. I entered a small waiting area, where two kids sat: one engrossed in a comic book, the other, staring into space, possibly slipping into a coma.

The door bearing Powell's name was ajar. I rapped twice.

"Come in," the smooth jazz voice said. I did as instructed. A chair squealed and a slim man with milk chocolate skin, warm brown eyes and a toothy smile rose to greet me. He looked to be in his mid-thirties.

"Let me guess," he said. "Sam McRae?"

"Good guess."

"It wasn't hard. What can I do for you, Sam?"

He motioned for me to sit. I showed him my client's release form—my former client, that is. The dead one. A quick wall survey revealed diplomas, a social worker's certificate, and personal photos, including a few of the school's sports teams.

"Let's start with Tina Jackson's disciplinary problems," I said.

Powell sighed, leaned back, his hands behind his head. "Tina was always a bit withdrawn. Kept to herself when she first came here. Like a lot of kids with issues at home."

I nodded and made a mental note to pursue that point further.

"Last year, the problems started. Lateness, talking back to teachers. Her grades slipped a little. What kind of legal trouble is she in?"

"Delinquency proceeding over a purse snatching. She accidentally knocked down the victim and injured her."

Powell shook his head. "I'm more than a little concerned about Tina. She's started hanging with a rough crowd." He picked up a file and flipped through it. "She was involved in a fight on school grounds. She's never been in that kind of trouble before."

"She hasn't been in any other fights?"

"According to the file, no. Not in the two years she's been coming here."

I nodded. This squared with what Tina had told me. So far, so good. "What happened? How did this fight start?"

Powell consulted the file. "It started between two girls, Lakeesha Robinson and Rochelle Watson. There had been friction between them. It finally erupted, I guess. You could say they're competitors."

"Over what? A boy?"

He hesitated. "This is going a bit beyond what's on the record."

"It could make a great deal of difference in helping Tina if I knew."

Powell appeared to think about it. "Well, don't quote me, but the word is, Lakeesha's head of a girl gang called the Most Wanted Hotties. Rochelle formed her own gang called the Pussy Posse. Lakeesha probably sees Rochelle as a threat."

"The Pussy Posse?"

He raised his hands. "I'm not making this up."

I shook my head. What it lacked in subtlety, it made up for in alliteration. "How do you know this? About the gangs."

"Mainly from the kids, though the security chief keeps an ear to the ground, too. Hell, some of the girls brag about what they've done. They're smart enough to keep it outside school, for the most part. But you'd have to be an ostrich not to know a few of them are doing heavy shit outside these walls." He gestured around with one hand.

A loud knock interrupted and a man poked his head in. I got a glimpse of a uniform under the light brown face.

"I'm busy, Greg," Powell said.

"Sorry, man. Catch you later." The door closed.

Powell smiled. "Even the janitor can be a source of information."

"So this was a gang fight?"

"If I were a betting man, I'd lay money that's why it started. Lakeesha felt threatened and decided to assert her dominance. Apparently, when Tina came to Rochelle's defense, the girls began beating Lakeesha up in earnest. Tina was part of the melee, unfortunately."

"And Tina's in this gang? Rochelle's gang, that is."

"If she's not in it, she may be trying to get in, based on what you told me."

"So the purse snatching may have been a kind of initiation?"

Powell nodded. "It's the kind of thing they might require for membership. A test to prove Tina's toughness to the gang."

I took a moment to absorb it. I understood why Tina hadn't seen fit to share details of the initiation rite. But the prosecutor would learn about it, if she didn't already know. The information wasn't helpful to Tina's case, but the gang connection explained Tina's behavior. I wasn't wild about the explanation, but there it was.

"You'd mentioned earlier that Tina's had problems at home."

"I know her mother's been through drug rehab and anger management. Tina lived with dad, while mom got her act together. Not an ideal arrangement, from what I hear, but one of convenience. Dad gave her a roof over her head and no discipline to speak of. Now, she's bounced back into mom's care and, from what Tina tells me about the hours Shanae Jackson works, 'care' is a bit of a misnomer. Tina's practically raising herself."

Powell clucked his tongue and shook his head. "It's sad, seeing Tina get into trouble like this. She's a bright kid who deserves better. You know that girl has an IQ of 135? When she started here, her grades weren't great, but they were good. They've been slipping ever since. It doesn't help that she gets no support at home."

"It gets worse," I said. "Tina's mother was recently murdered."

"No." His eyes registered shock. "My God. I hadn't heard that."

"I heard only yesterday," I said. Even news like that took a while to travel, it seemed. I handed him a card. "Thanks for your time."

"No problem." He gave me his in return. "Don't hesitate to call if you need anything else, Sam."

"Thanks, Frank." I shook my head. "Pussy Posse. Provocative name."

"They're at a provocative age," he said. "So many of our kids are sexually active by the time they hit twelve—even younger. A lot of them are having sex parties by that age, believe it or not. Many of them think nothing of slipping into a restroom or a closet to have oral sex."

"When I was in middle school, kids were either smoking or selling pot in the restrooms. Times have changed."

"Indeed they have," he said.

I got up. "Oh, one more thing." I felt like Columbo. "Do you know if Tina's here today?"

"I don't, but you could check with her home room teacher, Alice Fortune. Room 180."

"Thanks again."

He nodded and smiled. I made a mental note to keep
Frank Powell in mind as a future source of other information
Tina might conveniently forget.

CHAPTER SEVEN

I caught Alice Fortune, a short, stout woman with caramel skin and close-cropped black hair, in the middle of a class. I peered through the small window in the door. She read, while the kids bent over their desks in classic test-taking posture. When I tapped on the glass, she strode toward the door, her colorful dashiki-style dress swaying over ample hips. "Keep your eyes on your papers," she ordered before stepping into the hall.

"I'm in the middle of a class," she said, glancing at my pass. "If you have a problem to discuss—"

"I'm very sorry to interrupt. I have one quick question for you." I introduced myself and explained what I was doing there. "Is Tina Jackson in school today?"

As I explained my purpose for being there, her expression changed from irritation to deep concern. She paused and took a breath. "Tina hasn't been in school all week. I'm worried about that child," she said. "She's too smart to be involved in this kind of nonsense."

"I'm worried about her, too. Her mother was recently murdered."

Her hand flew to her chest. She gulped air, her eyes wide. "Lord, no." She shook her head and murmured, "That's horrible. Truly horrible. Mind you, I know the woman could rub a person the wrong way. But that's just tragic. Maybe that's why she hasn't been in school. I'm surprised no one told me."

"Thing is, her mother's body was discovered only yesterday, but you say Tina's been out all week? So she was skipping school before her mother died. And I take it you've met Shanae Jackson?"

"She came to one parent-teacher meeting. Never saw her at another. Tina said she had to work nights."

"What did she do to rub you the wrong way?"

"I'm not saying she did. I'm just saying she could. She was the kind to get attention because she complained a lot, you know? Not to speak ill of the dead, but it's true." She glanced back into the room to make sure the class was following orders. "I know she got up a full head of steam when she met with Mr. Powell and Mr. Thompson, after Tina got into that fight."

"Who's Mr. Thompson?"

"Reggie Thompson is the vice principal. I don't know if Ms. Jackson was madder at Tina or the school for making her come in. She acted all put out that they wanted her there. I mean, her daughter had been in a fight." The teacher spoke with a derisive edge that told me exactly how little she thought of Shanae. "Now, I know she probably slept late if she worked nights. Still, you'd think she'd want to be involved in something like that. Then, earlier this week, I heard she came back to see Mr. Thompson about something else. I don't know what that was about." She shook her head. "All I know is, Tina's another example of a good kid going bad. I see it all the time."

"You seem particularly concerned about her."

"She's brilliant, that's why." She gave me a hard stare. "She was in my English class last year. The girl could be an honors student, if she just tried." She emphasized each of the last four words with a force borne of frustration, sadness, and bitterness. "So many of these kids could be more than what they are. All I can do is try to make it interesting for them. They're the ones who have to do the work. Some of them do, others . . . ." She sighed. "The whole system makes it impossible to really teach them, anyway. This stupid quiz, for instance." She waved a hand toward the room full of kids. "All I do is teach them how to take tests. Do they learn anything from it? Sure—how to take tests. Some days, I feel like a damned glorified babysitter, you know?"

I shook my head, not knowing what to say. "How do you do it?"

"Hmm?"

"How do you do this?" I gestured toward the classroom. "Day in and day out."

She smiled but without mirth. "Well, it's not for the money and it's not for respect. So I guess it must be love."

"That's something, anyway. To love your work."

"Fools fall in love, Ms. McRae."

φφφ

For the umpteenth time, I tried reaching Tina on her cell phone. I left yet another message. Before leaving the school, I stopped by the office to ask about Rochelle Watson. Trying to get someone to look up her schedule proved futile. Frustrated, I returned to my office. The insurance company had called with a lousy counter-offer on Dancer Daria's slip-and-fall. The answers to my interrogatories in the messy divorce still hadn't arrived.

I wrote a polite, but firm letter to Slippery Steve, Esquire. Then I called him, only to be shunted to voice mail, where I left a message that he needed to get those answers to me or he could expect a motion to compel discovery—and soon. "Have a nice weekend!" I snapped before slamming the receiver down. "And you better spend it getting those damned answers together," I grumbled to myself.

My last business for the day was to call Walt with a report on what I'd learned since our meeting.

"So Marzetti may know something about this ITN account," Walt said. "Cooper as well. You think Cooper might be behind it? Maybe with some help from someone on the inside, like that Ana Lopez gal?"

"She could have been the one to plant the money," I said. "Ana works in the accounting department, so she's there all the time. And Ana could have gotten hold of Marzetti's access code and created the account." I sighed. "This is all speculation, of course. But there's no doubt that Brad is the only one currently authorized to create the account, and the money was in his file cabinet."

"But this thing with Marzetti—"

"I know. If Marzetti found a suspicious account similar to the one Brad discovered, it seems likely we're talking about the same account. Which would mean the account existed before Brad began working there."

"And Cooper did nothing after Marzetti told him about it? More than a little suspicious," Walt growled.

"Which would mean Cooper was involved too. Or . . . ."

"Or what?"

I shook my head. "I'm going to sound like a conspiracy theorist. What if Cooper raised the issue, but someone higher up chose to ignore it?"

"Why would they do that?"

"I don't know. Unless someone in upper management is part of the embezzlement scheme."

"If that were true, they could have set Brad up to take the heat off themselves."

"We're doing a lot of speculating here," I said. "We need to get some facts."

"We also need to keep after them about that audit." Walt's tone was brusque. "Plus, from what you're telling me, we need to get a computer forensics specialist in there to examine the system. We need to do it fast, before . . . ." He paused. "I don't know what, but we need to do it fast. You're making me paranoid."

"Since nobody's sued or prosecuted anyone yet, we can't even get a court order to examine the system," I said. "All we can do is pressure the company to do the right thing and try to find out what we can, however we can. Have you tried talking to Hirschbeck about this? Maybe he'll be more receptive to you than me."

"I gave Hirschbeck a buzz earlier today," Walt said. "He tells me Jones is arranging the audit as fast as she can. As for the computer forensics, he's balking. In any case, it all has to go through headquarters in Philly, but the audit's supposed to be in the works."

"Right. And the check is in the mail."

"I hear you. Thing that worries me is, if this does go higher than Cooper, maybe whoever it is will pull strings to make sure Brad stays on the hook for it." He paused. "If Hirschbeck's doing his job, he should eventually learn the truth, but you know how corporate counsel are sometimes. He may be lazy or turning a blind eye to his client's shenanigans. He might even be involved. You know this guy. Do you trust him?"

"Not entirely," I said. "We do have a history. I dated him while we were in law school. It ended ... badly."

"He dumped you?"

"No!" I blurted the word louder than intended. "I dumped him, after finding out that he snuck into our evidence professor's office and stole a copy of the final exam. While looking for notes from another class, I found it in his papers after we took the exam. When I confronted him about it, he acted like there was something wrong with me." The memory made me nauseated. "No, I don't trust him."

"Well, that's not a ringing endorsement, is it?" Walt said. "I take it your history hasn't made dealing with him any easier?"

"I guess he's pissed about how it ended. I knew I could never respect the man again. So I broke it off. I don't think he's ever forgiven me. Which is a hell of a thing, considering I did nothing wrong. I never ratted him out. You'd think that would be worth something to him. Jerk."

"Male pride," Walt said. "You took the high road, and he resented your implication that he wasn't good enough for you."

"Well, he wasn't."

"I can be the contact, if you'd prefer."

"No, Walt," I assured him. "I've dealt with difficult people before. It's part of what we do. I can handle this."

"I know you can. But if you keep hitting a brick wall with this clown ..."

I smiled. "I'll let you know."

"Good. So what's our next move, kiddo?"

"Stay on Hirschbeck about that audit, I guess, and push for them to check the computer system. Find out what Marzetti and Cooper know about this." I paused to think of more options, but little came to mind. "I could try to get Marzetti to go back to Kozmik and tell them about the account he saw in the system."

"Didn't Jon Fielding mention it to someone?" Walt asked.

"Yes, but that was second-hand knowledge. He didn't know all the details. If I could get Marzetti himself there, he could tell them what he found, which might move things along. Assuming he can remember. It's been more than a year."

"If push comes to shove," Walt said, "I say we go right to headquarters. They'll put the pressure on, if Hirschbeck continues to stonewall us."

Assuming there aren't accomplices at that level, I thought. Now I was getting paranoid.

"Speaking of Philadelphia, I was thinking of taking a trip this weekend."

"Oh, yeah?"

"Up to Philly, with a short detour to Frederick. A nice little road trip."

"Sounds like fun," Walt said.

"I haven't seen the Liberty Bell since I was in high school. And I could go for a Philly cheesesteak. The real thing."

"I've never seen the Liberty Bell," Walt said. "You'll have to tell me all about it when you get back."

"Will do."

"Enjoy your cheesesteak. Don't forget the Bromo."

CHAPTER EIGHT

Saturday morning was a good time to travel up I-270 to Frederick. The few cars on the road were probably leaf peepers heading to Western Maryland, avoiding a longer trip to Skyline Drive in Virginia. Any weekday morning, this stretch of road would've been jammed owing to area commuters living farther and farther from downtown D.C. With all the businesses springing up along the "I-270 Corridor," I'd heard that traffic was as bad heading out as in. Once again, I gave thanks for my two-block commute.

Marzetti lived in a new development just outside Frederick's historic district, cul-de-sacs with look-alike two-story houses. The term "suburban palatial" came to mind. Marzetti's house sported a brick facade with yellow siding and bright white trim.

The man who answered the doorbell appeared to be in his late twenties or early thirties, with a shock of red hair and sleepy brown eyes. He wore gray sweats and a faded blue T-shirt.

"Mr. Marzetti, I'm Sam McRae. I'm an attorney working for Brad Higgins. He took over your position when you left Kozmik Games."

"Right. So what's this about?"

"I'd like to ask a few questions."

A slim, dark-haired woman in jeans and an oversized top wandered over and placed a protective hand on Marzetti's arm. She gave me a curious look. "What's up?"

"Just something about my old job." He removed her hand and stepped outside. "This won't take long, honey," he called over his shoulder before shutting the door.

With a hand on my back, he drew me away from the house. So much for a tour of Marzetti's mini-manse. Maybe another time.

I stopped before we reached the curb. "Right before you left Kozmik, I understand you found a suspicious account in the accounts payable system. Was the vendor ITN Consultants?"

His brow furrowed. "I don't remember."

"Which don't you remember? Finding a suspicious account or the vendor's name?" I caught a glimpse of Marzetti's wife peeking from behind a curtain.

"Neither one."

"So you never spoke to your old boss, Darrell Cooper, about a suspicious vendor account?"

"I don't know. It's been a year since I worked at Kozmik. I can't remember everything I did while I was there. Why?"

I ignored the question. "I'm assuming that if you'd found a suspicious account, you would remember, wouldn't you?"

"I don't know. It wasn't my job to look for them. I just set up the accounts and paid the vendors. Darrell Cooper was supposed to keep an eye out for any problems."

"What problems in particular?"

Marzetti shrugged. "Excessive costs, lack of information on who ordered from the vendor, what they ordered. That kind of thing."

"So your job was confined to paying the bills?"

He nodded so vigorously I thought he'd get whiplash. "Right. You might want to ask Cooper about this suspicious account."

He turned toward the house. "But someone told me you *had* mentioned a suspicious account appearing in the system before you left," I said.

His eyes flashed anger. "Who told you that? Whoever did is a liar."

"How would you know? You said you couldn't remember."

He stopped short, wearing a deer-in-the-headlights expression. "You . . . you're trying to trick me. Put words in my mouth."

"No. I just want to verify that there was an account for ITN Consultants in the system before Brad came onboard. Nobody's accusing you of anything."

"Look, just leave me alone, okay? I don't know anything about any fake vendor," he snarled.

"I didn't say it was a fake vendor." I enunciated each word with care. "I said it was a suspicious account. Now, why don't you tell me what you know about this?"

Marzetti's eyes darted around. "Look," he said. "I don't remember an account—suspicious or phony or whatever you want to call it—and I don't know anything about this ITC or whatever they're called. And as for Kozmik, I'm through with that place. So you can quit wasting your time and mine."

He did an about-face and stomped toward Marzetti Manor.

φφφ

As I drove up I-95 to Philadelphia, I pondered Marzetti's reaction. Maybe, like Brad, he had stumbled across something he wasn't supposed to find. Odd that Marzetti, like Cooper, had left so quickly and so soon after discovering the problem. Had he planned on leaving or did finding the account have something to do with it? Perhaps someone—

Cooper?—had warned him not to tell anyone about the account. Cooper could have found a way to hack into the system and create the account. And, maybe, after Brad raised the alarm again, Cooper cut bait and ran, taking most of the money and leaving some of it behind to implicate Brad.

An interesting theory, but that's all it was. I needed hard proof.

It took me less than two hours to reach Cooper's place, a dilapidated row house in a shabby North Philly neighborhood. One of several identical iterations squeezed together. The building looked tired, as if the only reason it stood was the support from its twin brothers to either side.

I parked in an alley littered with old syringes, spent condoms and broken glass. As I climbed the stoop, I had to wonder: What's a former corporate middle-manager doing in a shithole like this?

I rang the bell. While waiting, I had time to consider if Duvall had led me to the wrong Darrell Cooper. Duvall had said this was a forwarding address. Maybe he was just having his mail sent here and living somewhere else. Then why not get a post office box?

I knocked and waited some more, thinking of cheesesteaks. I hoped I could get one far from this god-forsaken neighborhood. The door opened a crack.

A pale-faced woman with shar-pei wrinkles stuck her snout under the chain. The odor of cigarettes and B.O. drifted out. "Whatcha selling?" she asked.

"Nothing," I said. "I'm looking for Darrell Cooper."

"Really? Well, ain't he the popular one?"

"Does he live here?"

"Depends on what you call 'living.' He keeps his shit here and stops in from time to time."

"When did he move in?"

"Couple weeks ago." Right around the time he quit Kozmik, so it probably was the right Darrell Cooper.

"And someone else has come to see him?"

"Who wants to know?" She brought a hand up and poked a smoldering cigarette between her lips. "You a cop?"

"No. But I need to talk to him."

"Well, he ain't here right now." Her cigarette bobbed as she spoke. "Fact, I ain't seen him for two, three days maybe."

"So who else was here to see him? And when?"

She lifted her hand and rubbed her fingers together. "Fork it over," she said.

I gave her a twenty, wondering if it was enough. It seemed to please her. She took the cigarette in her stubby fingers and a cloud of smoke drifted from her mouth. She smiled, revealing a missing molar on the upper left.

"A big, bulky guy in a fancy suit come 'round. Had light-blond, buzz cut hair. He acted like a cop and I could tell he carried a piece." She patted the area just below her shoulder.

"A gun?"

"Naw, a piece of cake. Yeah, a gun. Whatta ya think?"

I soldiered on with the questioning, despite the odd feeling that I was starring in the Philadelphia version of *The Wire*, as written by Damon Runyon. "When was this again?"

"About three days ago, I guess."

"That was the last time you saw Cooper, right?"

"Right. Cooper didn't seem too happy to hear about the guy."

"Not happy how?"

She shrugged. "I dunno. Not terribly upset or nothin'. Just not happy."

"You said he was popular. Anyone else been looking for him?"

She nodded. "Yup."

Impatient with her monosyllabic responses, I struggled to maintain my cool. "And who was that?"

She lifted her hand and did another finger rub. I pulled out another twenty. This was adding up. I wondered how I'd describe it in my expense account. Research? Worked for me.

"Two times, a tall, skinny nigger come by looking for him. Yesterday and the day before. He was in a uniform, so the first time, I opened up. Thought he was UPS or sumthin', but I shoulda know'd it wasn't, cuz the uniform color weren't right. He was in blue, not brown."

"Like a blue jumpsuit?"

"Yeah, like that."

"Can you describe him?"

"Looked like a nigger. Just like any other."

"Long hair? Short? Light skin? Dark?" I tried to prod her to describe him in greater detail than just the N-word. It may have been too much for this woman. "Anything you remember?"

"I don't know. Brown skin. Dark eyes. Short hair." She ran through the description in a sing-song. "Just another—"

"Old? Young?" I said, before she could spit the word out again.

"Not old, not young. You can never tell with them people."

"Any distinguishing marks? A scar? A tattoo?"

She shook her head. "Nothing on his face but a damn smile. Least 'til I tole' him Mr. Cooper weren't here. I couldn't tell you about any tattoos. His arms and legs was all covered up." She sucked on the cigarette.

"How about the other guy? The big blond one. Is there anything special you can remember about him?"

"Naw, just what I tell you."

"Did either of these guys give a name?"

"Are you kidding?"

"Did either of them tell you anything about why they wanted to talk to Cooper?"

"Naw, and I weren't about to ask the big cop no questions. I just told him Cooper weren't here and the guy left." She snorted in a wet, throat-clearing way that made me wince. "Goodbye and good riddance to him."

"What about the black man?"

"He just said he needed to talk to Darrell Cooper. I said he wasn't in. He asked when was I expecting him back. I said I didn't expect anything because it wasn't my job to keep track of my tenant's comings and goings. I told him he'd have to try again another time and he go off, all in a huff. He come back again the next day, only I didn't open up this time." The crow's feet around her eye scrunched as she winked at me.

"So do you know where Cooper is?"

"No clue. Like I said, not my job to keep track of his comings and goings. I'm assuming he'll be back, though."

"Why's that?"

"All his shit's still here, that's why. He don't pay me for next month and it's still here, out on the street it goes."

"Ms . . . I never got your name."

"McKutcheon. Elva McKutcheon."

"Could I take a quick look in his room?"

She smiled. I had my wallet open before she could lift her hand.

CHAPTER NINE

I ascended steep stairs with Elva McKutcheon huffing ahead of me. The wallpaper was a faded rose print, but the place reeked of stale cigarette smoke and grease—hardly roses.

Elva opened the door and swept an arm, as if to say "Behold." I entered. The room was neat, furnished with utility in mind: a single bed, an old chest of drawers, a dresser with a microwave, hot plate and TV on it, a dorm-size fridge, and a small suitcase, open on the floor. I peered in. A jumble of men's underwear and socks. All the comforts of home.

In the bathroom, I found a clean sink, razor, miniature can of shaving cream and a bar of soap. I checked the cabinet. Half a bottle of Aqua Velva.

I started pulling out chest drawers, one at a time. Cooper hadn't bothered to unpack. In the third drawer, I found a file. I picked it up and rifled through it: copies of invoices from ITN Consulting. Interesting. Also, an envelope. Inside was a small, unmarked key. I wondered what it might open.

I tried the next drawer down. Empty. Elva shifted back and forth as she watched me. I felt her eyes follow my every move.

"Look," she said. "I know you said you wasn't a cop, but what's this about?"

"What do you care? You've been paid."

"Yeah, well, it's still my house. Lemme see some ID."

I smiled at her sudden interest in my identity and pulled out my courthouse badge. "There. Feel better?"

"Maryland State Bar Association," she read aloud. "You're a lawyer."

"No flies on you."

She scowled. She couldn't take it quite as well as she could dish it out. "You representing his ex-wife, right? The one he was bitching about owing child support to?"

"No."

"Sure you are," she said. "Else why'd you be going through his things? You're looking for money, right?"

I didn't know what I was looking for. I'd have been happy to find money, though I doubted Cooper would keep it in such an unsecured place. Clearly, the House of McKutcheon offered something less than Fort Knox protection. A bank book or account statements would have been helpful. Not for the reasons Elva had in mind, but to show that Cooper was an embezzler. Assuming I could link them to the fake vendor account.

"You said you last saw Cooper two days ago?" I asked.

"Two or three days. He'd been in and out anyway."

"Does he ever sleep over?"

"Don't ask me. If he does, he's quiet as a mouse. I never hear the faucet run or the toilet flush. Bed's always made. By the time I'm up, he's gone. He'll pick up his mail, spend time in his room now and then. I can hear him when he's here, making phone calls and stuff. But I think he's been steering clear o' here, ever since I told him about the big blond cop."

I turned to the dresser. One drawer held an appointment book. I flipped to the current month and started checking dates. The notation "10 P.M. No. 17" was written in pencil for the day before yesterday. Otherwise, the past two weeks were blank.

I kept up my search, Elva breathing heavily behind me, but found nothing of consequence.

"Ms. McKutcheon, I'm going to copy these," I said, holding up the file and address book, "and return them later today."

"Whatever you say, Miss Lawyer Lady. But 'tween you and me, your client is wasting her money."

"How's that?"

Elva snorted and looked at me as if I were a few cans short of a six-pack. "Let's face it. A guy livin' in a place like this obviously got no money. So how you 'spect him to pay any child support?"

"I don't," I said, hefting the file. Her face screwed up in a quizzical look, to which I said, "Thanks for your help. I'll see myself out."

She followed me to the top of the steps. "Blood from a turnip, Miss Lawyer," she called down. "You can't get it."

φφφ

The white guy who'd come to see Cooper wasn't a cop. A cop would have flashed a badge and identified himself. Maybe he was a private eye, hired by Cooper's ex to find him and serve him papers for back child support. Or Cooper could have quit Kozmik to impoverish himself—an attempt to avoid his support obligations and a bad move that would earn no sympathy from a judge. Perhaps Cooper had rented this dump as a mail drop instead of a box to throw people off his trail. Pretending to live there, while hiding somewhere else. But hiding from whom? His ex-wife? Someone at Kozmik? And why would he hide? If I could figure out who he was hiding from, maybe the why would follow.

In a better neighborhood, I found a cheesesteak and a Kinko's, in that order. I copied Cooper's entire calendar and the papers in the file, since answers might be buried anywhere in them. Another receipt for my taxes.

I toyed with the notion of having the key duplicated, but it was a plain key and I had no idea what it unlocked. What would be the point? I thought about keeping it and using it as leverage to get Cooper to talk to me. Tempting as that option was, it bordered on blackmail or behavior "unbecoming of an attorney." I cursed my ethical diligence and replaced the key in the envelope.

I returned to Elva's. She watched me put everything back where I'd found it. No sign of Cooper or anyone else since I'd seen her. I took a chance and left my card, offering yet another twenty for her discretion (to the extent it could be bought) and information on any new developments where Cooper was concerned.

With that, I headed back toward I-95 and home, hitting an ATM on the way. This had turned into an expensive trip.

At home, I fed Oscar, my 15-pound black-and-white feline companion, then decided to check my office voice mail. Maybe Fielding had thought of another important point, Marzetti had changed his mind about talking to me, or Elva had called with news worthy of all those twenties I paid her. The lone message was from William Jackson.

"Ms. McRae." The words came out jagged and anguished. "Please call me as soon as possible. They've arrested Tina. They think . . . they think she killed her own mother. It's crazy, but they do." There was a long pause, but for his ragged breathing. "Please call me when you get this. She needs your help."

CHAPTER TEN

Tina's indifference and bravado were absent in the Patuxent Detention Center's visiting area the following day. She sat hunched in a chair across the table from me, wearing a plain white T-shirt and jeans. She looked at me with wide, fearful eyes.

"I brought these for you," I said, handing over three young adult books I'd picked up at Books-A-Million in the Laurel Shopping Center, not far from my Main Street office.

"Thanks." Tina set them on the table, without looking at them. "When can I leave?"

"I'm not sure," I said. "There'll be an emergency hearing tomorrow before a master—as I explained before, a master's like a judge and decides certain kinds of cases. Anyway, he'll decide whether to release you to your father's care. I hope I can get you out, but it may be tough."

"Whatchoo mean, you hope?" Her voice rose a few anxious decibels.

"I mean you're facing some serious charges here. They may find you're a potential danger to the community, especially since you've already been charged with assault."

"But I din't do nuthin'."

"But they think you did and that may be enough for now."

Tina paused, her eyes filling with tears. "I swear, I din't do it. I wouldn't kill anyone. Why they think I'd kill my own moms?"

"I don't have the file yet. I'll get it first thing tomorrow, when they hold your hearing. I'll meet with you before we go into the courtroom."

Our meeting would be a rush-rush affair. I'd probably get an incomplete file and ten minutes tops to confer with her before the hearing. I could picture how it would go down—me, trying to discuss Tina's case and calm her nerves, while my stomach churned.

I'd take a standard approach—emphasize the good stuff about Tina, in hopes that the master would allow her house arrest with some kind of electronic monitoring. Not that I trusted Tina's father to keep her home, but the only alternative was detention in an overcrowded, understaffed facility.

"Let's talk about last Wednesday," I said. Shanae's body had been discovered Thursday morning by a neighbor, and from what William Jackson had told me, it appeared she'd been killed Wednesday night. "Did you see your mother at all that day?"

"Only in the mornin'. I was staying clear of her, 'cuz she was all up in my business. So most o' the day, I was wit' Rochelle."

"Rochelle? The one you defended in that fight at school."

"Right."

And leader of the Pussy Posse, I mentally noted.

"When you say your mom was 'in your business,' what do you mean exactly?"

"She always bitchin' at me. Like I can never do nothing right." She paused, then said, "She used to, I mean. Sometimes, when she like that, I jus' wouldn't go home. Or I'd wait for her to go to work first."

"I take it she worked most nights?"

"Yeah, mos' nights."

"How about last Wednesday? Was she supposed to work?"

"I dunno."

"Where were you that day?"

"At school, then I went to Rochelle's."

"Let's try that again," I said, recalling Alice Fortune's story that Tina hadn't been at school all that week. "And make it the truth this time. You skipped school that day, didn't you?"

Tina's mouth dropped open. "How you know that?"

"Never mind how I know. You skipped school all week, am I right?"

She looked up at me with wary eyes. "Yeah."

"What were you doing?"

"Jus' hangin' wit' Rochelle."

"So she was skipping, too? Every day?"

She nodded.

"What did you guys do?"

"Hung out at her place, watched TV, went to the mall. Whatever."

She must have been talking about Iverson Mall, which wasn't far from her house.

"Why didn't you go to school?"

She shrugged. "Jus' wanted to take a break."

"What did you do Wednesday? The mall or her house?"

"We was at her place. I did go by my house that morning to get some stuff, 'cause I wanted to stay at Rochelle's again that night. I figured I'd slip in while my moms was asleep, but she wasn't."

Tina's mouth curled down at the sides. "She see me and, suddenly, she be all in my face, yellin' an' callin' me worthless an' shit." Tears began to flow down her cheeks again and she swept them away with the palm of her hand. "Like she so much better," she added, in a tight voice.

Debbi Mack

"Did your mother ever hit you?"

"Sometimes, when she been drinkin'. She was a lot meaner that way when she was on crack."

"But she kicked that habit, right? And stayed clean?"

"I dunno. I guess so."

"Did she hit you that day?"

She shook her head.

"Tina, did you love your mother?"

She shrugged again. "I dunno. I guess. Ain't you s'posed to?" She turned a puzzled, anguished gaze my way. "I do know I din't kill her." Her voice cracked with sorrow. "Even if she din't love me, I wouldn't do that."

Her sorrow and frustration felt real to me, and I've dealt with my share of liars. Losing her mother was bad enough. Feeling like Shanae hadn't loved her must have been a crushing blow, made worse by her own ambivalent feelings.

"Tina, she was probably under a lot of stress, not only about you, but about money. Her job. I'm not trying to make excuses for her, but maybe she just wasn't good at expressing her love."

Another shrug. "Whatever."

"So that night, what did you do?"

"Like I say, jus' hung out in Rochelle's room watching TV. Some friends came over."

"You didn't go anywhere?"

She shook her head. "Naw."

"And Rochelle's mother didn't mind your staying over?"

"Rochelle's mother don't care about none of that."

It was time to ask the $25,000 question. "Is it true that Rochelle is the leader of a girl gang called the Pussy Posse?"

Tina froze. An eye twitched. "Who tole' you that shit?"

"A reliable source."

She paused. "I ain't never heard of them."

"Are you sure? Was the purse snatching an initiation rite for getting into the gang?"

Tina worked her mouth a bit. "I dunno 'bout no gang."

"This is important, Tina. I need you to be honest with me," I said, as forcefully as possible. "I heard Rochelle heads a gang called the Pussy Posse. Is this true?"

Tina shook her head. "I dunno."

Realizing that this dance could go on forever, I dropped the subject for the time being.

"You ever do drugs, Tina?"

"Naw," she said, her head bowed.

"Ever drink?"

She shook her head, eyes glued to her lap.

"Look at me," I said, putting some steel in my voice. "I get the distinct feeling you're not being straight with me. If I'm going to be your lawyer, you gotta be straight with me."

"That ain't the way I heard it."

"Then you heard wrong. When I ask you a question, I want to hear the truth. If it's the ugly truth, so be it. But if you lie to me and I'm blindsided because of it, you're not doing either of us any favors." I paused to take a breath and looked at Tina, who still wouldn't look back. "Now, gang or no gang, were you and your friends drinking or doing any drugs that night?"

"Ah-ight. We was getting a little high, yeah. But we just did some weed is all. Really."

If that were true—and that was a big *if*—I could believe she hadn't killed anyone that night. Unlike a drinker, a pot smoker was far more likely to steal a bag of Cheetos from a 7-Eleven than beat someone to death.

"And did anyone other than the girls and Rochelle's mom see you there?"

She fidgeted in her chair. "Naw. They the only ones know where I was."

"How about Rochelle's neighbors? Did any of them see you or stop by while you were there?"

"I dunno. I don't think so."

Splendid. My client's alibi could be backed by some friends, one of whom was the reputed head of a girl gang,

and all of whom were stoned at the time and might have any
number of reasons to lie for her. I made a mental note to
verify Tina's story with Rochelle's mother. Tina had already
lied to me about being at school and smoking pot. I figured
on talking to Shanae's neighbors, too, in case anyone saw or
heard anything that night.

"Do you know of anyone who would want to hurt your
mother?"

"I dunno." She shrugged.

"Did she have any boyfriends?"

Tina's mouth twisted into an ironic grin. "Little D weren't
exactly a boyfriend. He just a friend, but he'd come by a lot
to see her."

"What's his name?"

"Little D."

"Do you know his full name?"

"All I know is, Little D. He drive a sparkly green car with
fancy wheels."

"So . . . do you want to tell me anything else about that
night before I go?"

"Naw," she said, her eyes downcast.

"You never saw your mother that night?"

"No." Her voice was firm, unequivocal. "I was keeping
clear of her. I swear."

"And you definitely didn't kill her?" Even though she'd
already answered, I had to ask again.

"No! I did not kill my own moms." Her voice was harsh
with indignation. Tears welled. She was either giving me an
Oscar-worthy performance or she was just a confused and
upset 13-year-old, being wrongfully held for the murder of
her own mother.

She swallowed and fixed a solemn, wide-eyed gaze on me.
"So, my hearing tomorrow, right?"

"Yes. They'll bring you to the courthouse and, like I said,
I'll get to see you before court starts."

"And then I can leave this place?" She shivered and lowered her voice.

"I'll do my best, but I can't make any promises. This is murder we're talking about."

"Please. I gots to get outta here." Tina barely whispered, her voice ragged with emotion. Her expression radiated pure fear. "I'm scared. E'ryone here so mean. Girls walkin' 'round here with shivs made of toofbrushes and shit. An' the guards don't do nothin'."

"Hang in there, Tina. I'll do everything I can to get you home."

Even as I said it, I wondered what the word "home" meant to her. Did she really have a home with her father? I had reservations about Rodney Fisher's abilities in that role. Yet, I doubted she was better off in here. It was well known that juvenile detention facilities were poorly run and could be as dangerous as the worst streets of Baltimore. It was a depressing dilemma. It was my duty as her advocate to get her out, if I could, regardless of Rodney Fisher's failings as a father.

φφφ

Back at the office, thoughts of home led to a memory of a day at the beach with my parents. I couldn't have been much older than seven. As we traipsed across the hot sand, my mother's wavy blonde hair and tiny blue bikini turned lots of heads. She wore bright red lipstick, Jackie O–style sunglasses, and an infectious smile. My dad unfurled the blanket and planted a tattered pink umbrella in the sand with the authority of Admiral Perry staking a claim on the North Pole. He stripped off his yellow T-shirt to expose a pale, but healthy-looking set of pecs.

"Well, kid," he said. "Ready to hit the water?"

I shook my head no, knowing how cold that first contact would be, but he grabbed me and tossed me over his shoulder like a sack of grain. Carrying me kicking and squealing the whole way, he ran for the surf, plunged in, and waded to a point where he dropped me.

The shock from the cold water was like a slap. It may have been only a few feet deep, but I floated free. Murky sounds burbled around me. Instinct kicked in and I pushed to the surface, gasping for air as I broke through, my father's laughter ringing in my ears.

φφφ

Recalling the beach, with my parents alive and happy, caught me short. Grief washed over me in a way it hadn't since they'd died in a plane crash when I was nine. I closed my eyes, willing the image to dissolve. When I opened them, I was surprised to find my cheeks wet.

Backhanding the tears away, I focused on Tina again. She was the one with the problems—bigger problems than I'd ever faced.

I wanted to believe Tina, but doubt lingered in the back of my mind. Could she have killed Shanae? Could she be lying about that night? Shanae's beating was too extensive for self-defense. Or was it? If Shanae had been on drugs, a crack high could've made her violent. And very powerful. Someone using the bat in self-defense might have had to kill her to stop her.

This led to a disquieting thought. What if Tina had killed Shanae in self-defense, but was afraid to admit it? Even to herself.

CHAPTER ELEVEN

At the courthouse the next morning, I got my ten minutes with Tina—five minutes after getting her file. It didn't take long to figure out I held a "dummy file," something to show she was charged with a new offense, with nothing in the way of meaningful information. No police report, no school records, no intake forms—nothing. I entered my appearance for Tina at the hearing and flew by the seat of my pants with what little I had.

In a quick conversation with ASA Ellen Martinez beforehand, I'd been able to find out that the softball bat found next to Shanae Jackson's body had belonged to Tina and had Tina's prints on it, as well as Shanae's blood. A neighbor had also overheard Shanae and Tina arguing on the day Shanae died and other occasions. Since our last meeting, Martinez had been in touch with Frank Powell and some of Tina's teachers. Martinez learned about Tina's deteriorating attendance and disciplinary record. I noticed she didn't mention the Pussy Posse and wondered if she was holding it for later or if she wanted to check the veracity of the information before raising it in court. The prosecution had five days after I entered my appearance to disclose in discovery their evidence against Tina. I'd have to wait and see if the matter came up then.

I made all the arguments I could for house arrest and electronic monitoring. Despite my best efforts, the master refused to release Tina to her father. William Jackson stated that Fisher wasn't fit as a parent, only to have the master tell him Tina wouldn't be released anyway. The master said Jackson would have to file a petition if he wanted to fight with Rodney Fisher over his parental rights. Fisher yelled that it would be a cold day in hell when Jackson took his little girl from him. Things went downhill from there, and the bailiff removed Jackson from the courtroom. In so many words, the master told Fisher to behave or get thrown out, then he finished announcing his ruling: Tina was to remain in custody pending trial.

I put a hand on Tina's arm. "I'll request a review of the decision. Meanwhile, hang in there. I'll be by to see you as soon as I can." She wouldn't even look at me before they led her off.

With a sigh, I packed my briefcase. While I was in the neighborhood, I considered going by Ray Mardovich's office. The thought of airing a few grievances was both tempting and humiliating. My humiliation won out. I made a beeline for the door.

φφφ

I was heading back to the office when my cell started vibrating. I never drive and take calls at the same time—and I would like to personally crucify every idiot I see driving with a phone pressed to their ear—so I pulled over to check the number. It was Walt.

"Where've you been?" I asked. "I need to tell you about my road trip this weekend."

"I've been up to my ass in alligators," he said, his voice hoarse with fatigue. "The shit has hit the fan."

"What now?"

"Sondra Jones is dead. One of the office cleaning crew found her Friday night, shot in her office."

"You're kidding."

"Do I sound like I'm kidding?"

"Tell me this has no connection to the embezzlement and our client."

Walt was silent.

"Walt, you're not telling me what I want to hear."

"And I'm not hearing what you want to hear. Robbery wasn't the motive. Her purse was there, money and credit cards in her wallet. To make matters worse ... I don't want to talk about this on the phone. We need to meet. How soon can you be at my office?"

"Give me twenty minutes."

φφφ

When I got to Walt's, I gave him a quick rundown on the weekend before we turned our attention to Jones's death.

"The good news is," Walt said, "our client hasn't been implicated in this. Not yet."

"Thank God. The way you were talking—"

"Hold on, I haven't given you the bad news. Brad found the body before the cleaning crew."

"He found it? And didn't report it?"

"He said he was scared. He was supposed to meet Jones to discuss his employment status and the audit. It was after business hours and no one else was there. When he saw the body, he freaked and ran. He didn't want to get involved."

"Great. Now what? As far as Brad and the audit and all."

"I don't know. We should touch base with Hirschbeck on that."

"If he's as informative as he was last time, it'll be a short conversation. Anything else you need right now? Just so you know, I have another murder to defend." I filled him in briefly on Tina's case.

"If they do arrest Brad, I can be there for the questioning," Walt said. "I could use your help with fact-finding, identifying witnesses and so forth. Finding out who else was there that night and why anyone might have a motive to kill Jones."

"How about the real embezzler?" I asked. "Jones was an outsider. Her push for an audit might have threatened the actual embezzler. Since Brad knew he was under suspicion, I don't think he would have done it. He'd have to know he'd be a logical murder suspect."

"Sure," Walt grumbled. "If he was thinking logically at the time."

"Good point," I said. "Still, it's all the more reason to push Hirschbeck on getting this audit done." I paused before adding, "Assuming, of course, the audit clears him."

Walt raised his eyebrows, then said, "Yeah." I was trying to think of something reassuring to say, when the phone rang. Walt picked it up. "Yeah . . . . Yes . . . . Okay, where are you?" There was a long pause, during which Walt nodded and grunted repeatedly. "Okay, okay. I'll be right there. Don't say anything more 'til I get there."

He hung up. "That was Brad. Scratch what I just said about our client not being implicated." He pawed around on his desk and scooped up a legal pad and a pen.

"He's been arrested?"

"Not arrested, but held for questioning at CID. You know what that means."

"It means I've got to get to work. I guess someone must have spilled about Brad's meeting with Jones."

"Lobby security camera. Has him coming in the building's front door at 6:25 P.M. Right in the window of time they think she died."

φφφ

I returned to the office and put in a call to Hirschbeck, leaving a message with him to call back ASAP. I checked my mail. Still no sign of the answers to interrogatories in the wretched divorce case. I had, however, received another, slightly better, offer to settle Dancer Daria's slip-and-fall. The offer still stunk, but I stuck a copy in an envelope to mail to my client, out of obligation more than anything else. As for the interrogatories, it was time to file that motion to compel discovery. Between fighting for Tina's release, looking for evidence to keep Brad out of the slammer and forcing Slippery Steve to provide discovery information in the Divorce from Hell, I had plenty to keep me occupied.

While I was working, Hirschbeck called back.

"Your client's not going to get away with killing Sondra," he blurted. "The audit will take place."

"He's innocent until proved otherwise, Lenny. You do remember that much from law school, right?"

"We should have known this might happen." He continued to rant, as if I hadn't said a thing. "I should have insisted on being at that meeting."

"Who else knew about their meeting?"

"Why, our president and the department heads. They were all concerned about the audit and Sondra told them she was going to meet Brad and answer any questions. Clarify his situation, so to speak."

"You mean, let him know if he still had a job, while your company was dragged, kicking and screaming, through this audit."

"Now who's jumping to conclusions?"

"I'm just wondering why it's taking so long to get the show on the road. I mean, here you are, a small company owned by a large conglomerate. Things are running smoothly. No one from headquarters is bothering your operation and, suddenly, whoops! Turns out someone's been stealing from the till. You try to resolve the situation yourself and end up pointing the finger at Brad Higgins, who looks good for it, based on circumstantial evidence. When the big boys in Philly find out what's going down, they send Jones in to straighten things out and maybe get you guys to tow the company line. People start to feel threatened. Could be a motive for murder, yes?"

Silence at the other end. For a moment, I thought Hirschbeck had hung up.

"You should be more careful what you say," he growled.

"As should you. And, if I were you, I'd get that audit done—and fast. You should also have someone take a look at your computers, because I have reason to believe the accounts payable records have been tampered with. You need to take a closer look at who it is you're representing and how they're operating. It's quite possible that you're shielding an embezzler and a killer, and you don't even know it."

His heavy breathing told me he was still there, but not happy.

"Len," I said. "You should know that it doesn't pay to take shortcuts or turn a blind eye to the truth. I would have expected that you learned something since you cheated on that evidence exam. Maybe I wasn't doing the profession any favors by keeping that to myself."

"This isn't the same. I'm not the same." His voice was ragged and gruff. "I'm just trying to do my job."

"And you can't do it well if you refuse to find out what your client is up to."

"Don't you get all high and mighty on me. How closely did you look at your clients at the PD's office? Are you going to tell me every one of them was innocent? Keep your opinions to yourself."

A loud click told me he'd had enough. I sighed and hung up.

φφφ

The next day, while at the courthouse in Upper Marlboro to file my motions, I decided to drop off a copy of the motion in Tina's case at the State's Attorney's Office.

I spotted Ellen Martinez in the hallway, caught up with her, and pressed the copy into her hand.

"Hi," I said. "I'm contesting Tina Jackson's pre-trial detention. Thanks for saving me the stamp."

"I'm glad to see you. Do you have a minute?"

"Um, sure." Why did she seem so glad to see me? It was probably too much to hope that they'd found another suspect and were dropping the charges.

Martinez, who was her usual cool, immaculately turned out self, in a gray sheath and matching jacket, escorted me to a small conference room. She asked me to wait for five minutes. I took a seat at the long conference table. She returned and sat at the head of the table, crossing her legs in that self-possessed way of hers. Without fanfare, Martinez said, "Given the brutal nature of the crime, your client's possible association with a gang, and some other factors, we're going to ask that Tina be tried as an adult."

I sat a moment, not sure how to respond. I couldn't say it was a complete surprise, but I had hoped it could be avoided.

"If the court approves your request, doesn't that mean she'll be moved to the adult jail?"

Martinez nodded. "I'm afraid so."

"Is that really necessary? She's already scared to death to be where she is."

"Your client is manipulating you, Sam. She's not an innocent little girl."

"I know she's a tough kid, but she's still a kid."

She shook her head. "I'm afraid it's out of my hands."

The door opened and my former paramour, Ray Mardovich, walked in. The sight of him hit me like a punch in the gut. For a moment, I couldn't move. I stared at him and felt my chest tighten.

"Sam, you know Ray, of course," Martinez said, oblivious to how I glared at him.

Ray wouldn't make eye contact. He sat across from me, looking a bit worn around the edges. He seemed to have aged significantly over the last three months. The lines on his face were more deeply etched and his hair was more gray than brown. *Having a tough time keeping up with your little girlfriend?*

Ray straightened his tie, as if to show he meant business. "Assuming we prevail on our request, which I'm confident we will, I'll be prosecuting the case."

I kept quiet. Martinez coughed and rose. "Excuse me," she said, and without further explanation, left.

"So," Ray said. "You . . . look good."

"Cut the crap, Ray. I know about Amy."

To his credit, he blushed. "Yes, I suppose that was bound to come out eventually."

I had so many questions I wanted to ask, I didn't know where to start.

"Bound to come out? What were you waiting for? An engraved invitation to tell me?"

He shrugged, looking sheepish. "I didn't want to hurt you."

"Well, you did." My words underscored the shame I already felt. I thought about Ray's wife and how she had a legal right to feel hurt.

Ray stammered. "I know you're angry. Can we not make this about us?"

"I'm not mad." I spat the words. Affecting an offhand tone, I said, "I guess I just never gave you credit. Imagine having the energy for *two* extramarital affairs at once. That's amazing for a guy your age. You on Viagra?"

Ray shot me a withering look. "I'm not that old," he said, in an obvious bid to lighten the mood.

Old enough to be her father—almost. Again, I kept my mouth shut.

"Never mind all that," I snapped. "We have business to discuss."

Ray's shoulders relaxed and relief washed over his face.

"Let's start with why you want to try my client as an adult."

"Well, it's a brutal crime." Ray leaned back in his seat, as if settling into a hammock on a summer day. "And your client has possible connections to a girl gang."

"Possible connections. So you don't know for sure."

"We have reason to suspect she's connected to a gang."

"Based on what?"

"We know about the fight at school and her association with Rochelle Watson. We know the rumors about Rochelle. Of course, there's also the pending matter of that purse-snatching. We see these things as possibly being connected."

"Even if it were true—and I'm not saying it is—that doesn't mean Tina would kill her mother."

"No, but it might make Tina more likely to be violent toward her. We know there was a history of animosity—even physical abuse—between the two."

"What about Tina's father, Rodney Fisher?"

"What about him?"

"Shanae Jackson was going to seek additional child support from him, based on income he supposedly wasn't reporting to the IRS. Wouldn't that make him a pretty likely suspect?"

Ray stared off at a spot over my shoulder. "He'd have to be one cold-ass father. To beat his child's mother to death, then leave the bat at the scene to set her up. His own daughter? Why wouldn't he just shoot Shanae and ditch the gun?"

Well, some people can be pretty cold. About a lot of things. I forced myself to stay on point and respond in a businesslike manner.

"Maybe he didn't plan it. Maybe he came over and they argued and it just happened."

He frowned. "I suppose it's possible, but what about the fingerprints?"

"It was Tina's softball bat. Of course her prints were on it. The killer probably wore gloves."

"That sounds like planning to me. This looks unplanned—like a crime committed in the heat of rage. And it's hard to argue with the forensic evidence. Even if it was her bat, there were no other prints on it, except Shanae's. Oh, and there's a witness—"

"Yes, the argument on the day Shanae Jackson died. Ellen told me the neighbor overheard."

"Did she tell you that same neighbor saw someone she thought might be Tina leaving the house around the time of the murder?"

My heart sank, but I managed to keep my expression neutral. Was this another small detail Tina had lied to me about? "Really? What time was that, by the way?"

"The ME tells me she was probably killed between six and eight that night. Here." He handed me some papers. I shuffled through them. They included Tina's intake papers (essentially, a juvenile version of an arrest report), a preliminary autopsy report, and the neighbor's statement.

"It was dark, of course," Ray said. "So the neighbor didn't get a good look at the face, but she could see it was a light-skinned black kid, very thin and about Tina's height."

"So it wasn't a positive ID," I said.

"Right now, we have Tina's fingerprints on the murder weapon, no forced entry by the killer and someone who looked a lot like Tina leaving the house around the time of the killing." He stood up. "That, plus the history of bad blood and neglect and possible gang associations make Tina look good for this, I'm afraid." He glanced at his watch and turned toward the door.

"Wait!" I called, jumping to my feet and walking toward him.

He looked at me, and I could feel my heart melt. He must have seen something in my eyes, because he shook his head as I approached him. I could feel the electricity running between us.

"Sam, we can't—"

Before he could get the words out, I hauled off and hit him. I'd meant for it to be a slap, but somewhere along the line, my hand had balled into a fist.

The fist struck his nose and mouth so hard, we both yelped. I shook out my hand, pain coursing up my arm. Ray covered his nose with both hands, a wounded look in his eyes.

"You son of a bitch! That's twice you've hurt me." With that, I kicked him in the groin. Grimacing, he doubled over, fell to his knees and gasped.

I gathered my things and left without saying goodbye. I figured it went without saying.

As I strode down the hall, I realized how much my own actions supported his argument about how people act in the heat of anger. Anger I was forced to acknowledge now.

So much for keeping things businesslike.

CHAPTER TWELVE

I left the courthouse without running into anyone I knew (or, if I did, I never saw them) and returned to the office in a daze. The look on Ray's face after I hit him and the satisfaction of bringing him to his knees ruled my thoughts. I felt vindicated, yet scolded myself for acting so impulsively.

Back in my office I made a to-do list: talk to the neighbor who saw the kid leave the house the night Shanae was killed; try to confirm Tina's alibi; find out more about Shanae's friend, Little D; file appeals and motions. I made a mental note to call Hirschbeck ten times a day, or until he would give us something on that damned audit and agree to check the computers. I still wanted to find out where Cooper was hiding in Philly. If he was, in fact, in Philly. Those tasks, plus various and sundry other matters, would keep my plate full for a while. Full enough to push Ray into the far recesses of my mind.

I picked up the phone, then punched in Duvall's cell number. When he answered, I said, "How are the Carolinas?"

"Lovely, as always. I'd enjoy it more, if it weren't for this family business we have to take care of." He explained that they were cleaning out his mother's house before she went into an assisted living facility. Mom wasn't happy about it. I couldn't blame her.

He sounded tired and frustrated. I listened to him grouse and inserted a supportive "uh huh" now and then. Listening to Duvall's travails wore me out. I had my own shit to deal with.

When there was a break, I said, "Duvall, I hate to bring up business at a time like this."

"What do you need?" He sounded relieved.

"Can you recommend an investigator I could use while you're away? I tried to find Cooper at the Philadelphia address you gave me and struck out."

I recapped my conversations with Marzetti and Elva McKutcheon. My description of Elva made him laugh.

"Try Alex Kramer," he said. "She's in Baltimore. Her number's listed online. I've worked with her. If anyone can find Cooper, she can."

"Thanks. I've got too much going on here to find Cooper myself." I cradled the receiver on my shoulder and entered Kramer's name and city into Switchboard.com. "By the way, have you ever heard of a guy named Little D?"

"Little D? Sure. Got a lot of street cred, as they say. Don't tell me he has something to do with this embezzlement case."

"No, this is for another matter." I filled him in on Tina's situation.

"Little D's okay. I've worked with him whenever I've needed information from places in P.G. County where I ain't quite dark enough to pass for a local. See what I'm saying?"

"So he's a private investigator?"

"Well, technically, no . . . not licensed. He does favors for people, and he usually gets a little something for his efforts. He could help you find witnesses or do background checks for your murder case—unofficially, of course."

Oh, good, I thought. Another expense with no receipt. I pondered where to place it on my Schedule C. "Does this Little D have a name?"

"Darius Wilson, Jr. He's Little D and his dad's Big D."

"How far can I trust this guy?"

"Well . . . he won't double-cross you or do anything you specifically ask him not to do. He may use a few methods you don't like, but only when he needs to. You have to understand the kind of crowd we're talking about. They don't always respond to 'please' and 'thank you.' Tell him you know me. He'll treat you right."

"Okay. Long as he doesn't kill or torture people, I can live with that."

"Let's put it this way—I've never *seen* him kill anyone. And I don't think what he does qualifies as torture so much as persuasion."

"That makes me feel a whole lot better. Are we talking about breaking thumbs or kneecaps here?"

"He won't do it, if you specifically ask him not to." A low current of anxiety surged under my skin. *What would this guy do if you gave him no direction?*

"I'll have to watch what I say. Assuming I use him."

"I'd advise you to. Are you going to canvas the neighborhoods around Suitland all by your lonesome? I mean, some of these folks may have no problem talking to you. But if this involves a girl gang, there may be some you can't take on alone. When it comes to gangs, a lot of people require the gentle art of persuasion to start talking." Duvall paused. "And it never hurts to have someone looking out for your back. You've blundered into enough dangerous situations in neighborhoods where you wouldn't expect trouble, so why take any chances in this case?"

"Thanks for pointing that out," I said. My tone was acidic. I took a deep breath and forced myself to calm down. "I'll keep it in mind. Nobody in law school told me that my cases might require protection from a knee-breaker named Little D."

Duvall chuckled. "By the way, don't let the nickname fool you. Little D is anything but little."

φφφ

I chose to ignore Duvall's warning for now and visit Shanae's neighbor. Before going, I called Hirschbeck again and left another message. Maybe it wasn't fair to push so hard after the death of one of the company's own, but my first concern had to be Brad Higgins.

I drove to Hillcrest Heights where Shanae and Tina had lived. The neighborhood of small brick ranchers, paired by common walls, was off Fairlawn Street, not far from Branch Avenue and Iverson Mall—the kind of mall where you wouldn't find a Lord & Taylor or Nordstrom. A small lawn of half-dead grass and a stump fronted their house. I pictured tiny Shanae firing up a chainsaw and felling the lone tree. *So much for those damned leaves.*

I went to the house next door to Shanae's, a clone except that its owner had cared for it. Yellow chrysanthemums grew between a pair of azalea bushes, and a tall maple arched over the lot, its branches like protective arms. The house's brown shutters appeared freshly painted. A pot of purple and yellow pansies hung outside the front window. A faded green mat with "Welcome!" in white script lay on the front stoop.

I rang the bell and noticed a thin elderly black man raking leaves across the street. He stopped and looked at me then resumed raking. But I caught him shooting me sidewise glances.

A short woman with cocoa-colored skin opened the door as far as it would go with the chain in place and peered at me. She wore a yellow floral housedress and brown cardigan.

"Mrs. Mallory, isn't it?" I said. I handed her one of my cards. She looked it over with a slightly bemused expression. "I'm representing Tina Jackson. She's been accused in the, uh, unfortunate death of her mother."

"Dear God, tell me that isn't so!" The corners of the woman's mouth curled down and her brown eyes, like hot fudge sauce, gleamed. Worry lines furrowed her brow.

"Unfortunately, it is. I understand you saw Tina or someone who looked like her leave the house Wednesday night."

"Well . . . yes, I told the police that. But Tina wouldn't have killed anyone. I told them that too."

"What time did this person leave the house?"

"I think it was a little after eight. I'd drifted off in fronta the TV and a noise woke me up. People yelling. At first, I thought it was the TV, but no one was yelling on the program. So I got up and looked out the window," she said. "That's when I saw her."

"Are you sure it was Tina?"

"I couldn't be sure. But who else would it be, leaving her house at that time?"

"Did you get a good look at her face?"

"Not really." She squinted. "She wore a skullcap, pulled way low. The collar of her jacket was turned up, so it was kind of hard to see."

"What made you think it was Tina, if you couldn't see her face?"

"She was about Tina's height and her complexion was light, like Tina's. And, like I said, she was coming outta Tina's house."

"Maybe it was a friend?"

"I dunno. Tina don't bring too many friends over."

"What else was she wearing?"

"Kind of loose-fitting pants with the jacket. You know, what the kids like to wear."

"But you couldn't swear it was Tina. Are you even sure it was a girl?"

"Well, I couldn't swear it was Tina, no. But I think it was a girl. She was carrying a purse."

"Can you describe the purse? Did it look like Shanae's?"

She paused. "It was one of them satchel purses. I may have seen Shanae carry one, but then you see them all over, you know?"

I saw a ray of hope in this woman's lack of certainty. She couldn't positively identify Tina. And whoever it was could've been carrying Shanae's missing purse. Could it have been someone from the gang? It would explain the lack of forced entry, if one of Tina's friend's had asked Shanae to let her in. But why would a gang member want to kill Shanae? A chilling possibility crossed my mind. Surely, Tina wouldn't have *asked* someone to do it, or even paid them. These days, the notion of kids as hired killers wasn't beyond the pale.

"I'm sorry, how rude of me." Mrs. Mallory broke the silence following my plunge into morbid thoughts. "Why don't you come inside so we can talk."

"Actually, I didn't have much more to ask." But Mrs. Mallory had already scrabbled the chain off its groove and opened the door. She was a plump woman, with graying hair and a round, friendly face, its features only slightly eroded by time and the burdens of living. She gestured for me to come inside.

"Was there anything else you saw that night?" I asked, as she led me to a small living room. We sat on a sofa covered in nubby brown fabric. It sagged under our weight. "Anything at all?"

"Why no." She wrung her hands as she spoke, as if washing them. "I did see Tina come by earlier that day. I remember thinking she should've been in school. Then, I heard her mother yelling at her. These walls are thin. They argued quite a bit . . . ." Her voice trailed off and her expression turned wary. Her words were damaging to Tina. And she looked like she knew it.

"Could you hear what they were saying?"

She shook her head. "Not so I could understand it. They was both cursing a lot. But I couldn't tell you what it was all about."

"Anything else you remember about that morning?"

"Tina didn't stay long. They had words and she left."

"Did you see Shanae at any point after that?"

She nodded, still scrubbing her hands beneath an invisible tap. "I heard her talking to this man outside. He came by to visit in the afternoon. Some friend of hers with a fancy green car."

Little D, I thought. "When was that? Do you know how long he stayed?"

"Oh, I couldn't tell you. I just remember they were outside, talking. It was 'round four. She walked him to his car."

"You're sure it was four?"

"Yeah. I remember 'cause my stories were going off."

"Did you see Shanae at all after that?"

"Not alive. I was the one who . . . found her." Her lips pursed and her eyes were wet. "God rest her soul," she said, her voice cracking. "Poor woman. But I'm sure Tina couldn't have done such a brutal thing." She dabbed at her eyes with the back of her hand. "I know they didn't always get along, but Tina was a shy, quiet child. They had words, that's all."

I thought about Shanae's history of anger management problems and Tina saying alcohol fueled her mother's abusive behavior. It reminded me of the interviews you see on the news, after a murderer is caught. "I can't believe it," the neighbors say. "He was so quiet. So nice."

CHAPTER THIRTEEN

I knocked on a few more doors. Either no one was home or they weren't answering. I considered what Duvall had said about the barriers to finding information in this neighborhood. He'd given me Little D's number. I could probably afford to use him. William Jackson had agreed to pay me a healthy retainer plus expenses to defend his niece. Even so, I wasn't going to fork over money to have someone else do what I could manage on my own—at least, not yet. And, bad as this area was, how much worse could it be than Bed-Stuy in the '70s?

Rochelle Watson lived on the other side of Iverson Mall, in a cross-hatched network of streets near Marlow Heights Park. Another inside-the-Beltway enclave of old brick houses with big trees. The area wasn't much different than working-class neighborhoods in other parts of the county. Apart from low-end retail stores on the nearby highway, the prevalence of rust-bucket cars and the worn-around-the-edges look of some residences, you'd never know you were in the 'hood.

As I made my way up the walk, I had the familiar feeling of eyes focused on me. Eyes behind window shades and curtains. Two elderly women in porch rockers had stared as my car cruised by. I peered down the street, to see if they were still watching me. They'd probably gone inside to talk about me. Sure, and the CIA and the FBI were probably monitoring me through field glasses. My paranoia was becoming ridiculous.

The woman who answered my knock looked like she'd just rolled out of bed. And it was almost three o'clock. She could have worked—or possibly, played—nights. She had short, blunt-cut, black hair around a thin face with a sallow complexion. After establishing that she was Tanya Watson, Rochelle's mother, I introduced myself and asked for Rochelle. She took my card and blinked at it.

"Rochelle ain't here," she said, sounding listless.

"Tina Jackson says she was here with your daughter the night Shanae died. Can you verify that?"

"Shanae!" She snorted. "She lucky she lived as long as she did."

"She could rub a person the wrong way," I said, in a shameless bid to ingratiate myself.

"Heifer ain't gonna rub nobody anyway no more." Her eyelids drooped, as if she were fighting to stay awake. The cause was probably more than sleep deprivation. Tanya had the look of a heroin addict in mid-buzz. Her long-sleeved shirt probably hid track marks.

"Last Wednesday night. Do you remember if Tina was here with Rochelle and some friends?" I wondered what her memory would be worth.

I heard a toilet flush and an older woman, rounder than Tanya, came creaking down the stairs. She walked up behind Tanya and peered over her shoulder, making Tanya appear two-headed.

"My niece ain't feeling right," the older woman said. "Could this wait?"

"It okay, Aunt Louise," Tanya said, pronouncing it "ahnt" in that way that always sounds like an affectation to me. "I'll talk to her now." She widened her eyes, as if forcing them open.

Aunt Louise noticed the card Tanya held and snatched it from her. Looking it over, she said, "Well, if you gonna talk, why'on't you invite this lady inside?"

It felt like déjà vu. Gawks from the neighbors, followed by the once-over at the door, then an invitation inside. I began to regret my decision when I got a good look at the place.

Tanya didn't share Mrs. Mallory's neat-as-a-pin housekeeping ways. The women led me down a short hallway, its walls smudged with fingerprints and mysterious brown stains, to a living room crammed with furniture. Along one wall, a green velveteen sofa was wedged up against a blue loveseat, leaving barely enough space for a recliner upholstered in a variation of brown plastic. The Salvation Army rejects faced a large-screen plasma TV. Probably being paid for on the forever-and-a-day installment plan with no payments due the first year. Either that or the TV was so hot, you'd get third-degree burns if you touched it. Roaches scampered up the walls and made drunken circles near the ceiling. I glanced down and caught a few lumbering across the burnt orange carpet.

"Would you like something to drink? Coffee? Water?" Aunt Louise asked in a good-hostess tone.

"No, thanks. I'll keep this short," I promised. Real short. I perched on the edge of the brown recliner, poised to stomp any roaches that trespassed near me. "I had asked about last Wednesday. Were Tina and Rochelle here?"

"Yeah, they were. I saw them come in," Tanya said.

"What time was that?"

"Lemmee think. I think it was before dinner . . . ." Tanya's eyelids drooped again and she doubled over at the waist, nodding toward her lap. I looked at her aunt, who shook her head. She got up, grabbed Tanya's shoulders and maneuvered her into a reclining position on the sofa. Tanya offered no resistance. I rose to help and was rebuffed. Leaving Tanya to her narcotic dreams, Louise motioned for me to follow her into the kitchen. The dingy yellow appliances matched the curtains.

Louise lowered herself into a chair next to a speckled Formica-topped table. I took the seat near hers, averting my eyes from the roach convention on the counter and checking my immediate surroundings for strays.

"I've begged her to join a program," Louise said, "but will she? No. She keep shooting up that junk. All I can do is come by when I can and make sure she and the kids are okay."

You could report her to social services, I thought, but kept quiet. Louise might have viewed it as a betrayal, rather than a way to help Tanya. Besides, if Aunt Louise wasn't volunteering to raise the kids, who would? And who knows if they would be better off in the system than under the care of their own mother? From my brief observation, it appeared that Tanya was managing with her aunt's help.

Managing? My inner devil's advocate piped up. *You call that managing when your own daughter is in a girl gang?* But I could see the other side too. *How is taking her away from her mother going to change that?*

I squelched these thoughts and continued questioning the aunt.

"Were you here last Wednesday?" I asked. "Can you tell me if Tina was here with Rochelle and some other girls?"

"I was here, but I didn't get here 'til late. I come over and had to call 911."

"Tanya OD'ed?"

"No. She didn't take her insulin. She was fallin' out, like she was high, but it was cause o' not taking her meds. So I call 911 and went with her to the hospital."

I wondered if that was true or just a story for the medics. "What time was this? Did you see any of the girls?"

She shook her head. "I guess it was a bit after nine. And I didn't see no girls. If they was here, they was downstairs in Rochelle's room. But there's no way to know for sure."

"Why's that?"

"Even if they came home before dinner, whenever that was, if they was downstairs, they coulda left any time through the basement door."

Damn. Scratch one alibi.

φφφ

The sun was low in the sky when I left Tanya Watson's place. There was a chill and the acrid smell of burning firewood in the air. I started up the Mustang and sat shivering while the car warmed up. I should have brought a coat. Autumn, with its warm days and cool nights, always threw me off.

What now? It was too late to knock on more doors. Too late to visit people, too late to be in this neighborhood. Shit, my childhood neighborhood was worse than this. I looked around. In the gloom, the houses looked depressingly old. The big old trees seemed to harbor shadow and menace. I thought about Bed-Stuy again and wondered how I'd survived my nine years there.

I got to the office at six. Sheila, the receptionist for Kressler and Associates, the accounting firm where I sublet space, was packing it in for the day.

"You got a visitor," she growled. In her seventies, Sheila wore her gray hair in an efficient bun. She seemed to be growing increasingly terse with age. As if talking too much would squander whatever breath was left in her body.

"A walk-in? Haven't had one of those in a while."

"This guy said it was about a case you're working on." She squinted and lowered her voice. "He's a big, tall black man. Sound familiar?"

"I'm not sure." I thought of William Jackson. I wondered if he'd come by to make an in-person pitch toward his cause for becoming Tina's guardian. "Would you say he's in his late thirties or early forties?"

"More like mid-to-late twenties, if you ask me, but black people fool me on their ages all the time." She paused and added, "Oh, ex-*cuse* me. Make that African-American people." She rolled her electric blue eyes. "As if you ever heard one black person refer to themselves as such."

I laughed. "Thanks for letting me know."

"So . . . you want me to stick around?"

I know her question was well intended, but it grated. Was she asking because it was a man? Or because he was black? "No, no. Go on home."

"Okay," she said in her four-pack-a-day contralto and grabbed her purse. "G'night."

I wished her good night and tromped up the steps. My office door was open. I prefer it that way during business hours. I didn't want clients to feel they had to wait for me in the public area downstairs. Nothing had ever been stolen, so it worked out fine. I'd lock my office before leaving for the night, a mere after-hours formality—one more barrier beyond the front door for a would-be burglar.

I stepped into the office and understood Sheila's concern. A huge man sat hunched in my guest chair, dwarfing it. When he saw me, he unfolded himself and got up. He towered over me. Solidly built, his body was supported by tree trunks for legs. I wondered if he'd been a linebacker in a former life. He grinned as if he was pleased with himself; not in a threatening or condescending way. Damned if he didn't have freckles sprinkled across his coppery face.

"Sam McRae." His voice rumbled in the subwoofer range and he extended a hand which enveloped mine like a catcher's mitt. "I'm Darius Wilson," he said. "But you can call me Little D. I think you'll want to hear what I have to say."

CHAPTER FOURTEEN

"Well, Duvall was right." I said. "There isn't much truth to that nickname, is there?"

Little D issued a throaty chuckle. "A mere accident of birth order."

"Have a seat." I rounded the desk and sat down, while he wedged himself into the guest chair. "So what brings you to me?"

"I understand you're Tina Jackson's attorney." He made eye-to-eye contact. I liked that. "I want to help with her defense."

"How much would you charge?"

"Nothing." I must have looked surprised. "Shanae and I were friends," he continued. "I feel I owe it to her to look after the girl."

"You were just friends?"

He shrugged. "We did a bit of business, too. Mainly friends."

"When you say business, what does that refer to?"

"I'm getting to that," he said calmly.

I gestured for him to continue.

"First, let me just explain about Tina. I've met her and I know one thing—she may have done some bad things, but she's not a killer."

The prisons are crowded with people who "didn't do it," I thought. "How can you be sure?"

"Because I've met killers." His gaze hardened. "And she ain't one of them."

"I'm inclined to agree with you, but the police don't. And they have evidence to back their position."

"Such as?"

"Tina's association with a gang. The bat used to kill Shanae had Tina's fingerprints all over it."

He snorted. "'Course it had her fingerprints on it. I'm sure it had Shanae's fingerprints on it, too. When Tina quit her softball team, Shanae kept the damn thing around for protection, so either of them could've handled it. She also had a gun upstairs in her night table." He shifted in the chair, a brown bear trying to squeeze into a kiddie seat. "Ironic, isn't it?"

I let it pass. "Did Tina know about the gun?"

"Oh, yeah. Shanae wasn't too happy about having it in the house, but she felt like it was insurance. She kept it unloaded, the clip beside it in the drawer. And she warned Tina to stay away from it."

I rocked back and forth in my chair, considering that. "If Tina knew there was a gun in the house, why would she beat her mother to death with a bat? Unless she was uncomfortable with the idea of using a gun." I paused. "Or Shanae attacked her and she had to defend herself."

The way he squinted told me I'd never want to be on his bad side. "You think Shanae was still hitting on her? Roughing her up?"

"I don't know," I said. "I'm playing devil's advocate. The police know about Shanae's history of domestic abuse. That kind of abuse can become mutual over time."

He shook his head. "Like them social workers say, Shanae had some issues. Okay, so she wouldn't have won any Mother of the Year awards. But Tina's not a killer. She's a kid, just trying to fit in. What she needs is a little guidance. The kind of thing Shanae wasn't real good at giving. Why you think she started hanging with a gang?" he asked. "A gang's like family. What she didn't get at home, she tried to find on the street."

Again, I thought of Bed-Stuy. How differently things might have gone, if I'd stayed.

"You know, a neighbor saw what looked like a young kid, leaving the house late on the night Shanae died," I said. "Could have been Tina. Could have been a friend. She's not sure."

Little D pointed at me. "Maybe someone in the gang."

"Maybe. The neighbor didn't get a good look at the kid's face, so it might have been a boy."

His eyebrows knitted. "The neighbor give any description?"

"Whoever it was looked a lot like Tina. Around her height, thin. Light-brown complexion. Do you know if any of Tina's friends look like her?"

"I don't know many of Tina's friends," he said, then fell silent.

Nobody knew Tina's friends. Nobody saw Tina's friends. Did they wear invisible cloaks when they visited Tina? Or sneak in the back door while Shanae was working? Maybe they never went to Tina's house. Which would make it harder to argue that the kid at the house that night had been Tina's friend.

Dropping that issue for the moment, I said, "You were going to tell me about your business with Shanae."

His eyes widened and he appeared to refocus. "Right. Shanae had asked me to look into some of Rodney Fisher's business dealings."

"To get evidence for the child support case against him?"

He nodded. "I started looking into it, asking around. I hear that Fisher's been selling drugs, doing loan-sharking and money-laundering on the side." He drummed his fingers on one knee. "If Shanae was going to win her case, she'd need more than the word on the street to prove it. That's why I broke into the shop."

"Ah. And what did you find?"

He picked up a thick file from the floor and handed it to me. "Found some tax returns that say what he's supposed to be making. And a ledger that says what's really coming in. Some checks signed over to the pawn shop, too. I copied everything I could."

I flipped through the photocopies. One set of papers, held with a clip, were the tax returns. Another set, handwritten ledger entries. A list of names with cryptic notes was on the left; columns of numbers on the right.

"That's yours to keep," he said.

"Too bad Shanae doesn't care about child support anymore."

"Yeah, but when Shanae found out what he was doing, she was none too happy. And she was no shrinking violet. She told me she demanded he pay up, or she'd take him to court. And you know, if any of this shit came out . . . ." He whistled.

"So Fisher had a definite motive for killing her?"

"Look that way to me."

"When did Shanae tell you this?"

"At her house, the day she died." His mood was somber. That he made no secret of having been there relieved me.

Fisher was sounding more like a promising suspect than ever. If he'd gone to the house and had an argument with Shanae, maybe that was what woke up the neighbor, Mrs. Mallory. He might have grabbed the bat in anger and beaten the life out of Shanae and, in a panic, failed to dispose of the weapon. But then what about fingerprints? And who was the kid Mrs. Mallory saw leaving the house? Could she have mistaken Fisher for Tina? Didn't seem likely.

Scanning the checks, I halted abruptly when I noticed one for $5,000 made out to ITN Consultants. I blinked and stared at it. The check had been drawn from the Kozmik Games account. *Hello!* The back of the check bore an illegible signature.

Stunned, I tried to process this bizarre coincidence. Little D had just mentioned loan-sharking and money-laundering. Could the embezzlers have been laundering the stolen money through Fisher's pawn shop and signed the check over to him? It was sloppy, but even the most sophisticated criminals could get sloppy. Hell, the Watergate investigation started with a cashier's check intended for Nixon's re-election fund, which ended up in a burglar's bank account. I scanned the handwritten records, ordered by date, searching for a notation for ITN around the time the check was written. I found the entry, with "$5,000" entered next to it; "$500" and "$4,500" were written in the right-hand columns. I flipped back a month and found ITN again—this time with "$7,000" next to it. In the right-hand column: "$700" and "$6,300." It looked like Fisher was getting a ten percent cut. But where was the rest going?

Little D was still talking. "I'm kind of hooked into that scene. That's how I know him."

"I'm sorry. I drifted off. Know who?"

"Dude named Narsh. Worked as a drug runner for a while. Fisher got him acting as—what do you call it?—liaison between his clients and the shop. An enforcer, too."

"So he should be able to tell us who Fisher is dealing with."

"He should. Why?"

"Because it looks like Fisher is handling a transaction that involves a phony company. Something related to another case I'm on. I'd like to know who's behind that company."

"I can ask Narsh about it when I see him."

"You're going to talk to Narsh?"

"How else we gonna verify all these rumors about what Fisher been up to?" He leaned forward, hands on his knees and said with a sly smile, "Ain't you been listening?"

"Sorry. I got a little distracted looking through the records." I switched gears to Tina's case. "You think he'll talk to you?"

"Oh, he'll talk to me." Little D beamed confidence. "Eventually."

His smile made me nervous. "You think Fisher had Narsh kill Shanae?"

"With a baseball bat? Hired killers don't beat people to death."

"It looks more like a crime of passion," I said. "Unless that was the intent."

Little D shrugged and shook his head. "Nah. Too subtle. If Narsh was hired to kill Shanae, he woulda just capped her ass."

Little D's tendency to alternate between the Queen's English and street slang was amusing. A cross between a Rhodes Scholar and a gangsta rapper. Just the kind of guy I needed to help me with this case. "If you're going to talk to Narsh, I want to be there."

"This may not be the friendliest discussion. Be better if I handled it and got back to you."

"No," I said. He stared at me, as if I'd spoken a foreign language. "I want to meet him. Look at him while he answers the questions. Size him up for myself. Not that I don't trust you. There are just some things I have to do myself."

Little D leaned back and smiled. "Damn, girl. Well, all right. You want to meet Narsh, I'll have to take you to him, 'cause he ain't gonna come to you. And we're talking about Southern Avenue, babe. So you *will* want me to be there."

I thought about that decaying stretch of road, dividing the worst of D.C. from its mirror image in P.G. County. "Yeah," I said. "I will."

116

CHAPTER FIFTEEN

With no client meetings or court appearances, I wore jeans and an old long-sleeve pullover to the office the next day. Casual dress seemed in order for a trip to the 'hood. Though I had other work to do, my thoughts were stuck on Little D's promise to take me that afternoon to meet Narsh at a local bar serving as his office. My cases kept me occupied, but anticipation charged through me.

For the umpteenth time, I called Hirschbeck and got his voice mail. I left another message for him to arrange an audit and check the company's computers for tampering. I was beginning to feel like a parrot.

The deeper I got into the Higgins embezzlement case, the more certain I was that our client was getting hosed. I had no clue what to do about it. Brad Higgins hadn't been fired, so we couldn't sue for wrongful termination. And, as an "at-will" employee, I didn't see how we could sue Kozmik even if they let Higgins go. Still, I had to do something. For the moment, that "something" was to stay on Hirschbeck like a yellow jacket on a picnicker.

Walt called to tell me Higgins was a free man, for the time being. The police seemed suspicious, he said, due to Brad's appearance on the security video. Walt thought the cops might try to get a warrant to search Brad's condo. I updated Walt on my conversation with Little D—the records he'd found and our plan to see Narsh. I also told him about hiring Alex Kramer to find Cooper while Duvall was out of town.

"Maybe Cooper knows something about the pawn shop connection," Walt said.

"I hope so." I thought back to my conversation with the lovely Elva McKutcheon. "There was also a black man in a blue jumpsuit looking for Cooper in Philadelphia. Maybe it was Narsh or Fisher."

"Whoever it was may be able to identify the real embezzler."

"I hope to find out more from Narsh today."

"Good luck," Walt said. "I'll keep you posted on Brad's situation."

I hung up and went to meet Little D out front. The weather was still mild. A breeze showered colorful leaves onto the ground and sent them scampering down the street. I found their rustling soothing, like the patter of gentle rain.

I'd been in bad neighborhoods before—my childhood home in Bed-Stuy being the worst by far—but times had changed. Today's 'hoods made those of the past look pretty tame. Having Little D as a guide would help, but even he couldn't guarantee safe passage through the war zone shared by D.C. and P.G. County. The area had a reputation for harboring perps who evaded the law by crossing to the other jurisdiction. Cooperative enforcement was a work in progress.

Despite the risks, I won't delegate some work, like questioning people for information that might make or break my cases. I had to question Narsh face-to-face and judge his answers for myself.

At a couple minutes past three, Little D pulled up, his green Lexus sparkling, chrome wheels spinning and shining. Sliding onto the tan leather seat, I said, "Nice car to be driving in such a crappy area."

"Don't matter," he said. He turned to me. "Don't nobody mess with my car."

"You sure everyone on Southern Avenue got the memo on that?"

"If they didn't, they gonna hear it from me personally, after I find their sorry asses." He hunched over the wheel, his oversized frame filling the space, already scoping the streets for would-be car thieves.

φφφ

Southern Avenue, with its tiny houses, liquor and convenience stores, and gas stations, depressed me. Most houses had barred windows, reminding me of mini-jails.

Calvin's Bar was so dark, I had trouble seeing. But my nose didn't fail me. It smelled like the morning after a frat party—stale beer, cigarette smoke, and bodily fluids assaulted my nose. I held my breath. My eyes adjusted to the low light, and I noticed a few people in booths along one wall. A middle-aged man, round-faced and chestnut-complected, stood behind the bar having a loud conversation with two younger men—and possibly the rest of the neighborhood. At the far end of the bar, one customer slumped with his head on his arm, appearing not to hear.

"So I told that motherfucker," said one man in a Dallas Cowboys jacket, "I said, look here, you insult my peoples, you insult me. You gotta step off. You know what I'm saying?"

"Sheee-it. What he do then?" said the smaller man. His pants hung so low, he flashed his Fruit-of-the-Looms to the world.

"He try to get up in my face, but I slapped him around and he back off like the little whiny-ass bitch he is."

"You lucky he weren't carrying," the bartender said.

"That bitch be carrying my size-twelve boot up his ass, if he try that shit wit' me again."

Raucous laughter rang out. Little D stepped up to the group. I hung back, a few feet behind him.

"Excuse me, gentlemen." Little D's deep voice carried loud and strong over their laughter. The three men snapped to attention. "Calvin, could I speak to you a moment?"

The Dallas fan and Mr. Ass Crack looked up, then glanced at me. Their eyes met and they snickered. The bartender, who I assumed was Calvin, said, "Who the white girl, D?"

"A friend. I need to speak to you. Alone."

The men looked Little D up and down. Neither seemed anxious to argue with him, but neither moved.

Calvin flicked his hand and said, "Give us a minute." They slid off their stools and slouched away.

"Narsh been here?" Little D asked.

Calvin's gaze darted from me to Little D. "Ain't seen him lately."

"You sure 'bout dat?" Smooth as a gunslinger pulling a pistol, Little D dipped in his pocket and pulled out a fifty-dollar bill.

Calvin gazed at the fifty like a hungry man eyeing a juicy steak and gestured with his shoulder. "Who wants to know?"

Little D chuckled. "C'mon, Calvin. Don't start pretending you give a damn."

"Ain't a po-lice thing, is it?"

I stifled a laugh. "Do I really look like an undercover cop?" I said. "I blend in here about as well as David Duke at the Million Man March."

The corner of Calvin's mouth turned up, then broadened into a grin. "Who *are* you then?"

"I'm a lawyer, but that's neither here nor there."

"You planning on suing Narsh?"

"No." Not anytime soon, anyway.

"Well . . . ." he said.

Little D waggled the bill at him, ready to withdraw it at a moment's notice.

"Narsh hangin' at Choochie's now," Calvin said. "Just inside the District line."

"I know the place."

"Then you know he might be hard to reach, once you get there. And they ain't gonna like your friend."

"We'll see what we can work out. Thanks, Cal." He handed the fifty to the bartender and the two did a grip-and-slide handshake.

"So," I said, as we walked out. "What up, dawg?"

"Niggah please," he said. "Too white for words." His shoulders shook with soundless laughter as we walked to his car.

On the way to Choochie's, he said, "This could be a problem. You should probably wait in the car."

"Nuh-uh. I'm coming in."

Little D opened his mouth to protest. "I've got to talk to Narsh myself," I said. "I've come this far. And I'm going to see him."

His mouth snapped shut for an instant. "Fine. Wear my jacket. And there's a ball cap in the back seat. Put it on and pull it down low over your face. You have real short hair, anyway. With any luck, you'll look more like a guy—or at least a little less white."

I reached back and found a burgundy-and-gold Redskins cap. "Got any brown shoe polish?"

"Say what?"

"It worked for Gene Wilder in *Silver Streak*?" I grinned.

He smiled and shook his head. "You trippin', girl, you know that?"

CHAPTER SIXTEEN

Choochie's turned out to be an upscale version of Calvin's. The booths were cushioned in red Naugahyde, the air was less than aromatic, and the place had a dim glow. The few customers were male, black, and ranged from young to middle-aged. Rap blasted from a jukebox. Little D's jacket hung halfway to my knees. I felt like a kid playing dress-up. As we approached the bartender, I pulled the cap down until the bill practically touched my nose.

"Lookin' for Narsh. You seen him?" Little D asked.

The bartender, rail-thin, with crepey skin, gazed at Little D with blank brown eyes. "Ain't seen no one," he said.

"Next time you don't see him, be sure and tell him Little D lookin' for him. We got some bidness to discuss. About his employer. And a murder."

The bartender raised an eyebrow, but said nothing. He glanced at a hallway leading to the back of the bar.

"We'll be in the booth over there." Little D cocked a thumb toward the far corner, then grabbed a bowl of pretzels before walking to the booth. Soon as we sat down, the bartender vanished.

Little D nibbled a pretzel. "Shit, these mothers are stale." He threw it back in the bowl.

Debbi Mack

"Thanks," I said. "That's the last time I eat bar pretzels."
Little D grinned.

The bartender reappeared, followed by another man wearing a red do-rag. Short and well-built, his jeans molded to his well-muscled legs. His skin-tight T-shirt showed off bulging pecs. The bartender returned to his job and the muscle man continued in our direction. My stomach clenched.

"Whatchoo want?" he barked at Little D.

"Narsh, isn't it?"

"Why the mutherfuck I be talkin' to you if I wasn't?"

Little D replied in an even tone. "We have some questions for you about Rodney Fisher."

"What this got to do wit' murder?"

"I don't know yet."

"Well, if you don't know, I sure the fuck don't either."

The rap song stopped abruptly. A sappy ballad took its place. Narsh started to turn away. Little D said, "Then let's talk about something else."

"What?"

"Fisher's business."

"What make you think I'll answer?"

"Because I asked nicely." When Little D stood up, he towered over Narsh.

Narsh narrowed his eyes and snorted. "Ast nicely. You funny, big man. Well, the bigger you are, the harder you fall, mutherfucker."

"Just have a seat," Little D said. The voice of reason. "And talk to us."

"Fuck you." Narsh started to walk off. Little D grabbed his shoulder and Narsh swung at him with his right fist. But Little D was light on his feet for a big guy. He blocked the punch with his arm. Narsh swung again with his left, but missed when Little D ducked out of reach. Narsh tried again with his right. Little D sidestepped the punch, grabbed Narsh, and flipped him onto the floor.

124

Narsh lay there, shaking his head and looking like he didn't know what hit him. In the background, the jukebox diva was stretching the word "love" out to four syllables.

"Well done," I murmured.

"Tai chi," Little D replied. He offered his hand to Narsh. "Ready to talk now?" he asked.

"Sure, sure," Narsh said. He scrambled into a crouch. As he rose, I saw him reach into his jacket pocket.

"D—" I said. But Little D had seen the move. He grabbed Narsh's wrist, twisted his arm behind his back. A large handgun thudded to the floor.

"Muther . . . fucker!" Narsh arched backward, his face contorted in pain. "Let me the fuck go!"

"If you're ready to talk."

"Okay, okay. Shit."

Little D let go. Narsh rubbed his wrist and glared.

Extending an arm toward the booth, Little D said, "Have a seat." He picked up the gun, checked the chamber, removed the clip, and handed the empty weapon to Narsh. "You get the rest back after we get some answers."

Narsh slid into the booth, opposite me, and Little D sat beside Narsh, who looked quizzically at my face beneath the cap.

"More tai chi?" I said, feeling more at ease.

"Nah. Sometimes brute force is called for." Little D removed bullets from the clip, then glanced at Narsh. "I'll start. You do a lot of business for Fisher, don't you?"

"What if I do?"

"A lot of business ain't exactly legal."

"What if it ain't?"

I placed a copy of the ledger in front of Narsh. "Can you tell me who these people are?"

Narsh squinted. "Look, I dunno nothin'. I'm jus' a runner, see? Even if I knew, I can't be going around talkin' about it."

"But this does represent income Fisher hasn't claimed, doesn't it?"

"You with the IRS?"

I shook my head.

"Then whatchoo care, bitch?"

Little D dropped the clip. His hand shot up and clamped Narsh's neck. "You will use a polite tone when addressing my friend," he said.

Narsh made a choking noise. Little D withdrew his hand. Narsh inhaled sharply, then coughed, rubbing the sore spot.

I took another tack. "Do you know where Fisher was last Wednesday night?" I asked.

"No," Narsh croaked, still coughing. Little D pocketed the bullets after he'd emptied the clip.

"Where were you last Wednesday night?"

"Here, probably."

"Probably?" I was tired of this verbal dance. "C'mon, it was only last week. I'm sure you can remember back that far."

Little D gave Narsh a warning glare. Narsh, still rubbing his neck, said, "I was here, okay? Damn."

Assuming that was true and someone saw him here, Narsh had an alibi for Shanae's murder. But Fisher was still a suspect. I glanced at Little D to see if he had anything to say. He gestured for me to continue.

"Do you know Shanae Jackson?" I asked.

"She the mother of Rodney's chile, right? I seen her." Narsh's expression told me this wasn't a good thing.

"Did you see Rodney and Shanae argue any time recently?"

"She come by the shop and made a lotta noise, yeah. She do that now and then. Pain-in-the-ass bitch."

"You won't have to worry about her anymore. She was beaten to death."

His eyes widened. "You don't say?" He paused before speaking again. "With that mouth on her, can't say I'm surprised."

I wondered what it was he had chosen not to say. "She was murdered last Wednesday night. Do you know where Fisher was that night?"

He shook his head. "You po-lice or what?"

"Let's just say I'm an interested party. And it's really interesting that Shanae was murdered after the two of them argued so much. And no one can account for where Fisher was that night."

"That don't mean he killed her."

"Sure, but that doesn't make it any less interesting. Did they argue about money? Because Shanae thought Fisher owed her child support."

"I dunno. I just handle his business."

"His money laundering business?"

"I just make deliveries for the man."

"Do you know who this is?" I pointed to the ITN entry.

Narsh looked and shook his head.

"You must know who you're delivering to," I said. "Who is this?"

Narsh shrugged.

Little D put his hand on Narsh's arm. "Answer the question."

Narsh glared at Little D, who returned an unblinking gaze. "And why the fuck should I?"

"Cause if you don't, I'm gonna drag you outta this booth and kick your sorry black ass." Little D paused for effect. "Then, I'ma go to Rodney Fisher and tell him you sold us this information"—he pointed to the copy of the ledger—"and you'll be outta work and your name'll be dirt on the street. You be lucky to get a job at Church's Chicken as a gotdamn counter boy."

Narsh's mouth opened a fraction. His eyes were heavy-lidded and wary. "And if I talk, what's to stop you from doin' that anyway?"

Little D grinned like the Cheshire Cat. "Because then you're useful to us, and why would I want to hurt someone useful to us?" He shifted on the seat. "Either way, it'll save you an ass-whoopin'."

Narsh fell silent, likely weighing the consequences of his response.

"Look, I dunno names. All I know is two white boys."

"Two white guys?" I said. "Young? Old?"

"Young. Geek-lookin' mutherfuckers."

"So how does it work? They give you money and what happens next?"

Little D squeezed Narsh's arm. "We'd appreciate all the details."

Narsh swallowed hard. "I pick up the money from the white boys in the parking lot at Calvert Road Park and take it to Fisher. Now and then, I deliver some of that money to some 'bama give me a package. I take the package back to Fisher and he hold it 'til the white boys pick it up."

"Drugs?"

"Naw. Somethin' flat. Like a disc maybe."

I shot Little D a quizzical look. He shrugged.

"How often do you do this?" I asked.

"Maybe once a month, I get the money. The white boys pick up the package every two months or so."

"How long has this been going on?"

Narsh squinted and counted on his fingers. "It been about six, seven months."

"So who gives you the package?" I said.

"Don't know his name. Some niggah in a blue uniform."

"A blue uniform?" I thought of the black man who'd been looking for Cooper at Elva McKutcheon's place in Philadelphia. "Where do you meet him?"

"Iverson Mall."

"Are you meeting him anytime soon?"

"This Friday."

In two days. "When are you supposed to make your next delivery to the white guys?"

"This weekend. Saturday."

I looked at Little D. "I have an idea."

CHAPTER SEVENTEEN

It was a simple plan. On Friday, Little D would observe the Iverson Mall drop and follow the man in the blue uniform. Narsh would meet the white guys around twelve-thirty the next day in the lot at Calvert Road Park and give them their package. I intended to be there to see the handoff, take photos, and follow the two men after they left the park. Little D and I would touch base later that day.

Little D returned Narsh's empty clip and we left Choochie's. I asked if he would run me by Rochelle Watson's house. I still hoped one of the neighbors would confirm Tina's presence the night of the murder. Little D took me to the house. While I knocked on Rochelle's door, he visited other neighbors.

The door opened to reveal Tanya's thin, sallow face. "What is it?" Her eyes were as dull as her voice.

"Hi, Tanya. Remember me?"

"Yeah, I 'member you. Whatchoo want now?"

"I wondered if I could speak to Rochelle."

Tanya turned her head and, in a voice that could pierce steel, yelled, "Rochelle! Com'ere!" She turned back to face me.

"You knew Shanae Jackson," I said. "I assume Rochelle also met Tina's mother." Maybe Shanae had gotten up in Rochelle's face enough to threaten the girl or her gang.

"You have to ask her." She bellowed Rochelle's name once more.

Tanya opened the door wider. I had no intention of entering the Roach Palace a second time. I heard noises and a tall girl, well-developed for 13, in jeans and a skin-tight pink shirt emerged from the kitchen at the end of the hall. A pink-sequined scrunchie was wrapped around her wrist—similar to one Tina had worn in her hair the day she came to my office. Rochelle swaggered to the door and looked me over. Her pores exuded 'tude. "This lady here to talk to you," Tanya said.

"Yeah?" Rochelle said.

I introduced myself, explaining my connection to Tina. "First, I'd like to ask you where you were last Wednesday night."

Rochelle's eyebrows drew together. "What I have to do wit' this?" Tanya appeared to lose interest and wandered off.

"It may be important for Tina's defense."

"I was here."

"Was anyone with you?"

"You mean like Tina?"

"I mean like anyone."

She paused before speaking. "Tina here. And some friends."

"Members of your gang, the Pussy Posse?"

"Sure."

"So you are in a gang by that name?"

"Yeah." She leaned against the door jamb, arms akimbo. "I started it," she said with pride, as though speaking of the local Junior League chapter.

"Did your gang have any problems with Tina's mother?" I asked.

"We ain't had no problem wit' her, but she had problems wit' us."

"She didn't want Tina hanging out with you?"

"Somethin' like that. But Tina made it pretty clear she didn't give a shit what her moms want."

"Why is that?"

"Tina said her moms always bossin' her around. Heifer always trying to tell her what to do when she couldn't even keep her own shit together."

"So Tina decided to join your gang? Was it her idea?"

"I tole' her she could join and she say yes. What else she got going?" Rochelle gave me a knowing look. "Wit' us, she had a place to stay and friends to watch her back."

"Was the purse snatching her initiation?"

"Right."

Rochelle's nonchalance about her gang activities was quite a contrast to Tina's refusal to admit to them. "Is theft a regular pastime for you guys?" I asked.

"We do what we want." She stood up straight and bore into me with a hard look. "We gots our things we do for money, so nobody tell us what to do."

"Your mom know about the gang?"

"Shit no. Half the time, she don't even know what day it is."

"So Tina was here with you last Wednesday. All night?"

She paused again, then nodded. "Yeah."

"All of you."

Rochelle fiddled with the pink scrunchie. "Tina spent the night. The others left."

"What time?"

"I dunno. Late."

"Eleven? One in the morning?" My exasperation grew. Nailing down a few facts with this kid was like nailing Jell-O to a wall.

"I don't know." She came down hard on each word.

"What are their names?"

"Why it matter? You jus' want an alibi for Tina right?"
"Did I say that?"
"Well, what else would it be?"
"Who were the other girls?"
She smiled and shut the door in my face.

φφφ

Little D was waiting for me in the car. "No luck on the door to-door," he said.
"Why am I not surprised?"
We spoke little as he drove me back to the office. It was rush hour and traffic inched its way northbound on Route One. I stared out the window, catching glimpses through the trees of a MARC train rattling by, heading from D.C. to Baltimore.
"I wonder what's on them discs," Little D said.
My thoughts shifted from Tina's case to Brad Higgins's. "I was wondering that myself. Some kind of data? Trade secrets or confidential information?"
"Whatever it is, it obviously ain't for the good of their employer."
"Maybe they're using the information to set up their own business." I shrugged. "I don't know. Whatever's on those discs, these guys are stealing tens of thousands of dollars to pay for them."
We crept up on the light at Contee Road.
"Let me ask you something," I said. "You're one of the few people I've met who's had a good word to say about Shanae. How'd you get to be friends?"
He cleared his throat. "We had a kind of . . . business relationship."
"Dare I ask the nature of the business?"
"I met her back when she was dealing."

"Oh." His candor was refreshing. "Were you buying or selling?"

"She was selling and I was her source. When she got busted, she did me the favor of not turning me in. So I'd like to do her the favor of finding her killer."

"And that's why you're doing all this? As a posthumous favor to Shanae?"

"I told you. Tina is basically a good kid. And she deserves better. Why else?"

I didn't know, but my gut said there was more to it.

φφφ

Sheila had taken off by the time I got to the office. A stack of mail waited for me. I hauled it upstairs, separating wheat from chaff as I went. I spied an envelope with the divorce interrogatories. Flipping through the pages, I groaned at how often the defendant refused to answer a question—and on the flimsiest of grounds. I tossed them onto the desk and rubbed my temples. Ahead lay the torturous process of negotiating with Slippery Steve— making a "good faith" effort to work out our differences— before we took our dispute to the judge. Judges enjoy resolving discovery disputes—especially in divorce and custody cases—about as much as scrubbing toilets with a toothbrush. There has to be an easier way, I thought.

On the plus side, I'd gotten a decent offer to settle the "bruised knee" case. I called Daria the Dancer, who whined that it wasn't millions. I urged her to consider taking the more-than-reasonable amount, reminding her that she wasn't permanently disabled, proving negligence would be near impossible and, if it went to trial, she'd end up with bupkes. The McDonald's "hot coffee" fiasco and celebrity cases aside, I was incapable of arguing that Dancer Daria would be the next Twyla Tharp if not for her spill at Safeway. I copied the offer and sent it to Daria with a bid for her final "yea" or "nay."

I was updating my calendar and my to-do list when the phone rang.

"Sam." Walt sounded both discouraged and tired. I felt a pang of guilt. I was supposed to be doing the heavy lifting for him. "Brad's been arrested for Jones's murder."

"When?"

"This afternoon. The cops found a gun in his apartment and they think it might be the murder weapon."

I slumped in my chair. "What did Brad have to say?"

"He thinks someone planted it. He doesn't own a gun."

"Like someone planted the money in his office." I hoped the cynicism in my voice wasn't too obvious.

If it was, Walt ignored it. "Brad's bail hearing is tomorrow morning. Can you come to my office in the afternoon? I want to start planning our strategy."

"Sure." I filled him in on the meeting with Narsh and the plan to find out who was behind the ITN transaction. Walt sounded happy to hear the news and was more upbeat when we hung up.

A few moments later, the phone rang again. This time it was Hirschbeck.

"You're there late," I said. It was almost 6:30 by my watch. "I always thought you corporate attorneys were strictly nine-to-fivers."

"Meetings," he said, tersely. "The audit's in the works. Our Philadelphia headquarters gave us the green light."

"Great," I said. I decided to keep mum about the connection between the embezzlement and Fisher's pawn shop. I wanted more information about the nature of the deal and who was handling it on Kozmik's end.

"I'll let you know when I hear more." He hung up before I could ask if the computer records would be checked for tampering.

I needed to follow up with the investigator looking for Cooper. I got on the phone to Alex Kramer.

"You just saved me a call," Kramer said. "There's good news and bad news. I'll start with the bad. I found a real address for Cooper, at a friend's place. I guess he rented that cheap little room as a smokescreen. It's a moot point now."

"Why's that?" I asked. My gut told me I already knew the answer.

"A young couple taking a walk by the Manayunk Canal found Cooper. Washed up on the bank. He didn't look well."

CHAPTER EIGHTEEN

The news of Cooper's death took the wind out of me. I felt lightheaded. "When was this?" I murmured.

"They found Cooper yesterday," Kramer said. "The body was a mess. He'd been in the water a week or so, and that's just the ME's best guess, according to my sources. He was hit on the head, but the body was so discolored, it was hard to tell whether it happened before or after he died."

"Any call on whether this was an accident, suicide, or homicide?"

"At this point, it could be any of the above, though suicide by drowning is rare, as you know. No apparent signs of struggle. But with so much time in the water, it's hard to tell. He could have fallen in the canal and hit his head or he could have been beaned and dumped in the water. They'll know more after they check his lungs. And no one can say where the body entered the water. They may get a general idea, based on the estimated water flow rate. Pinpointing the exact location is a long shot."

"You mean he could have been floating downstream a while?"

"From the looks of him, he was submerged most of the time. Given our warm fall weather, it could have taken from a few days to a week for the body to surface. Or so they tell me."

"And the cops are still investigating?"

"That's the word. Now, here's the good news."

"I could use some good news. What is it?"

"When we spoke, you mentioned finding a key at that rat trap Cooper used as a mail drop. When I found out where Cooper lived, I snooped and found a fireproof box. Guess what? You need a key to open it. Maybe the one you found."

I sucked in a deep breath. "I take it you found it before the cops got involved."

"The day before. Talk about good timing. Anyway, I took the box to the office and forced it open. It had loads of goodies in it. I know you'll want to see and hear it all. I'll copy everything and send it to you before I turn it over to the cops."

"Hear? Are there recordings?"

"Yep. You'll see. A lot of the conversations mean little to me. They may mean something to you. I suspect Cooper was keeping them as insurance. It appears to be damaging information. I'm on a surveillance today, but I'll copy it tonight and send it to you first thing tomorrow."

I exhaled the breath I'd been holding. "Thanks, Alex. I appreciate your work on this. I can't wait to see what you found." I gave her my address and asked her to overnight the package the minute she could. "Let me know if you learn any more about how Cooper died," I added, before hanging up.

I checked my files and found the copy of Cooper's calendar. He'd made the cryptic entry "10 P.M. No. 17" for last Thursday, two days before I'd tried to find him. Was it an address? An apartment number? It suggested a meeting, perhaps Cooper's last.

I flipped farther back through the calendar and saw entries for "staff meeting" at regular intervals, a couple of doctor's appointments and what appeared to be personal information. Things were looking unremarkable until I noticed "6 P.M. No. 44" written on an April day. What was up with the numbers? I hoped the answer was somewhere in that fireproof box. Cooper couldn't tell me a thing now.

φφφ

The next day, Brad Higgins and I sat in Walt's conference room, while Walt fiddled with his VCR. The machine whirred as he ran our copy of the security tape forward and backward. The lobby camera in the building Kozmik Games called home was positioned at an angle high above and several feet back from the entrance, allowing an unobstructed frontal view of everyone who passed through the door. People zoomed in and out, in a blur. When we got to the segment about an hour and a half before Brad entered the building, Walt hit **Forward**, and we watched it play at normal speed.

Walt had arranged Brad's pre-trial release by convincing the judge that Brad was neither a threat to the community nor a flight risk. Walt emphasized that Brad was on administrative leave due to an employment-related situation. He assured the judge that Brad had every reason to stay in the area. The judge accepted the argument and allowed Brad's release on bail. I wondered how much Walt's argument had weighed in the judge's decision. Or had the judge merely acquiesced to the wishes of his frequent drinking buddy. The two were fixtures at a pub near the courthouse.

Brad gazed at the screen, looking dazed and dejected. On the tape, people paraded in and out. He recognized several Kozmik employees leaving between 5:00 and 5:30. The next half hour revealed nothing new.

A little after 6:00 P.M. he said, "Hold it." Walt hit **Pause**. Brad sat up straighter and made counterclockwise circles with his hand. "Uncle Walt, run that back, could you?"

Walt did so. A large man backed out of the building.

"That guy," Brad said, pointing at the screen. "I need to take a closer look."

Walt ran the tape forward at normal speed until the man's image filled the frame. He paused it.

Brad's eyes narrowed. "Yeah. That's him. I don't know who he is."

"You've seen him before, though?" Walt asked.

"Yes. At the office."

"Any idea what he might be doing there?" I asked.

Brad shrugged. "I saw him once or twice in the hall. But I'd never forget that face."

I took a good look. His mug would leave a lasting impression on the blind. Buzz cut blonde hair covered his block of a head. About six feet tall and bulky, his shoulders extended from Maryland to Ohio. And he wore a menacing look that said *Don't mess with me*.

There was something familiar about his looks that I couldn't put my finger on.

"So just 'cause this guy showed up on a tape doesn't mean he killed Sondra," Brad said. "Anybody who worked at Kozmik could be on that tape."

"True. But most of the employees had left by the time this fellow showed up," Walt pointed out. "And he isn't a Kozmik employee, is he?"

"We have a lot of employees." Brad shook his head and became pensive. "I can't swear that he isn't. I only saw him a couple of times. He may have done business with the company."

Walt laid a comforting hand on Brad's arm. "It's a start. We'll tell the police. Maybe it'll provide a lead."

Brad asked if he could go. After he'd left I said, "Given the fact that the weapon was found in Brad's condo, don't you think we need something stronger than Brad's word about this man? Maybe someone can identify him and tell us what he was doing at Kozmik."

"Good point. Maybe Hirschbeck knows something. In the meantime, I still think it's a good idea to alert the cops. Don't you?" Walt nodded as if anticipating my affirmation. "By the way, thank you for not mentioning the need for evidence to back Brad's story in front of the kid. He's shaky enough already."

The kid's in his mid-twenties, I thought. Old enough to understand we might need more than his word to keep him out of the big house. But he wasn't my nephew, and Mrs. Higgins wasn't my sister. And it was Walt's case. I saw no harm in playing it his way. Up to a point.

Walt knew someone who could produce photos from a single frame and do it stat. Once I had the photos, I'd show them around. "Let's set up a meet with the detectives and the state's attorney ASAP."

"Are you sure we want a big meeting so soon?" I asked. "How about if I call and share this with the detective on the case."

Walt, who'd been gathering his papers, stopped abruptly. "I want to make sure they don't blow off this evidence. This character could be a significant lead in the case."

"Or he could be nothing. It wouldn't hurt to know more about him. Especially since we're relying entirely on the word of the accused."

Walt's eyes widened. I read fear in his expression. "You think Brad is lying?"

"Walt, you've practiced criminal law for—what?—forty years or so? I don't have to tell you that it doesn't matter what I think."

Walt frowned. "You're right." He brushed the matter aside with a sweep of his hand. "I'm sorry. This case has me a bit wound up. My sister's worried sick. Brad's upset. I think it's getting to me."

"No problem," I said. In his shoes, I imagined I'd feel the same.

φφφ

After our meeting, I returned to the office. I decided to check on Vince Marzetti up in Frederick before I called Hirschbeck. I looked forward to hearing his reaction when I told him his former boss, Cooper, was dead. He answered on the first ring.

"This is Sam McRae. We spoke outside your house last Saturday."

"I remember. And I still have nothing to say."

Before he could hang up, I said, "Darrell Cooper's dead. Maybe murdered."

A long pause. "Jesus. No."

"Yes. That makes two Kozmik Games employees who've been killed in the past week or so. One was murdered. The other's death is highly suspicious. And I think it has something to do with that ITN account you claim to know nothing about."

"Two people dead?" Vince's voice was barely a whisper. "Look, I don't know anything about it, okay?"

"When you worked for Kozmik, do you remember ever seeing a tall, well-built man with blond hair?"

Marzetti fell silent.

"Does he sound familiar?" I said.

"No!" His voice rose. "I have no idea what you're talking about. Don't call me anymore." The conversation ended with a loud click.

Well, I'd gotten a reaction—but no information. At least, none that I could use.

I called Hirschbeck. To my astonishment and joy, he answered.

"Len," I said. "I have reason to believe the ITN account was created shortly before Brad Higgins started working there, not two months afterward, as the computer records say." I left Jon Fielding, my source, out of it, since Hirschbeck had such a bug up his butt about my talking to Kozmik employees.

Hirschbeck grunted. "Sondra told me one of our employees mentioned a strange account in the system before Higgins came on. I've asked the financial auditors to verify the account's purpose," he said.

So Hirschbeck already knew but had been playing it close to the vest. How could I blame him? I'd have done the same. "I'm thinking it's not another account, but the same one. Someone went into the system and changed the dates to set up Brad. The only way to verify it is to hire a computer forensics expert to determine if the computer records were altered and, if possible, by whom." Faint hope stirred in me that he'd see the logic in this.

He grunted. "Hiring a computer expert is an expense we hadn't anticipated. First, we have to justify it with headquarters."

Damn. More corporate hoops to jump through, I thought. "If the auditors find only one suspicious account—and I think they will—you'll still face the question of whether that account was created after Brad came on or it's the same one your employee mentioned, and it was altered to implicate Brad," I said. "That would be grounds for examining the computers."

For a long moment, he was silent. "You're right. I guess we'll have to wait and see what the auditors find. Got any other expensive suggestions?"

"No, but I have a question," I said. "There's another potential suspect in Sondra Jones's murder. Possibly a Kozmik employee or someone who's done business with the company. Tall, blond, huge—and hard to forget. Does he sound familiar?"

"Not really."

"He was caught on camera entering and leaving the building on the evening Jones was murdered, about a half-hour before Brad Higgins arrived. You're sure you've never seen someone like that, at a meeting or in the hall?"

"I haven't, but that doesn't mean much. We have eighty-five employees. I don't know every one of them. He could've been doing business with any of them."

I suppressed a sigh. "Do you keep photos of your employees on file?"

"No." He sounded brusque and defensive. "You could contact Personnel," he said in a calmer voice. "See if they've hired anyone matching that description. Otherwise, you'd probably have to check with each department head. If he's not an employee, someone may know why he was here."

I groaned under my breath. Going from department to department would beat interviewing eighty-five employees, but it would eat up the clock— and shoe leather. Seeing no alternative, I said, "I'll start with Personnel."

φφφ

Hirschbeck gave me the number for a woman named Kendall in Personnel. She spoke with a Midwest twang, lots of hard A's. When I described the hulk, she grew animated. "Gosh, it's been quite a while, but I remember. You don't forget someone that big. And mean-looking. I thought he was creepy."

"You hired him?"

"No, no. He came by, asking for one of our departments. In Personnel, we get a lot of people asking where so-and-so is. You know? I guess 'cause our office says 'Personnel,' right on the door. So they figure we know how to find anyone."

She giggled. Didn't seem that funny. Maybe she'd smoked weed on her last break.

"Did he mention his name?"

"Oh, no. He wasn't chatty at all. He just asked where he could find . . . . Darn, I can't remember. I do recall that his request struck me as unusual . . . ."

"Why?"

"Well, other than his lack of social skills, he didn't seem the type to be interested in . . . . If I could just remember what he was looking for . . . ."

"Accounting?" I asked, trying to prod her memory.

"Um, no, no. That wasn't it. Marketing? . . . no . . . ."

"Something to do with finances?"

"No, no. Not financial. It was something that didn't fit his looks, know what I mean? Usually, they're more . . . nerdy. That's it! It was . . . game development."

"Game development?"

"Yes, I remember thinking, he didn't look like a computer game developer. They're usually wimpy and wear glasses." She giggled again.

Game development. And the embezzled money was being used to purchase something on computer discs. Stolen programs for computer games maybe? Another piece of the puzzle fell into place.

φφφ

After I hung up with Kendall, I finished transcribing notes from our conversation and reviewed what I knew so far. When I got to the conversation with Elva McKutcheon, I slapped my forehead. Could the blond man have been the one looking for Cooper? The one Elva thought was a cop because, in her words, "he carried a piece"?

If Blondie was a hit man, why was he looking for Cooper? Was Cooper his client or his quarry? Did he knock Cooper out and dump him in the canal to make it look accidental?

I got up and began straightening and putting away files. Paperwork often took over my shoebox office. Doing something with my hands helped me clarify my thoughts.

Assuming Cooper was murdered, who would want him dead? Could it have been his partners in crime, if he was in on the embezzlement? Maybe they got greedy and decided to off him. Did Cooper sense this? Did he leave Kozmik knowing they were out to get him?

I stopped to look out the window. Dead leaves gathered at the bases of the street lamps and inside the iron tree guards around Main Street's Bradford pears.

Had Cooper posed a threat to someone because of Brad's discovery? When Brad discovered the phony vendor, Cooper might have decided to take the evidence to headquarters, in exchange for cutting a deal for himself. Come clean and avoid prosecution.

It would explain why Cooper had copies of the incriminating papers and why he rented at Elva's. Too bad it didn't work. But it didn't explain the cash in Brad's file drawer. An embezzler might have set Brad up and then dispatched Blondie to make sure Cooper never talked.

It was obvious that high stakes were involved. A bundle had been stolen to buy discs. People were dying because of what was on those discs. I wished I could ask Cooper about it.

CHAPTER NINETEEN

Like a pebble thrown into a pond, Cooper may have left some ripples—some evidence of his intentions. The contents of the fireproof box would soon be in my possession. Alex Kramer said the papers looked like "insurance" that Cooper was keeping as evidence of what the embezzlers were up to. If my hunch was right, Cooper had gone to Philadelphia for more than a cheesesteak. Perhaps he approached the parent company to cash in his policy, so to speak.

I got online and looked up the parent company, Mid-Atlantic Entertainment, Inc. Before dialing, I jotted notes of what to say and a list of responses to questions they were likely to ask. After listening to a litany of choices, I pressed "0" for a human being—a woman who spoke in a high-pitched, nasal whine. I explained that I was a lawyer, interested in speaking to someone about a matter concerning their Kozmik Games subsidiary. I reviewed my crib notes as I spoke.

"Can you tell me about the specific matter you wish to discuss?" the grating voice asked. "I want to direct you to the right person."

"I'm representing a Kozmik Games employee who's been placed on administrative leave, pending a financial audit. I

Debbi Mack

believe his supervisor, Darrell Cooper, may have contacted someone at your office to discuss something germane to the audit."

"Does this concern active litigation?"

"No." *Not yet.*

There was some hemming and hawing. "I'll direct you to Garland Perry, the vice president who handles that subsidiary." She gave me a four-digit extension, in case we got disconnected, then said, "Hold please."

I visualized what a guy named Garland Perry would look like and wondered why on earth a parent would choose such a moniker for a son. I repeated my story to an administrative assistant who put me on hold a moment, then patched me through to a man. His pleasant, bland voice told me he was bound for a lifetime of service in middle management. I pictured someone of medium height with a soft midsection and thinning hair, possibly a comb-over.

"A lawyer, eh? I'm not sure I'm supposed to be talking to you . . . ."

"If I promise not to use any Latin words, will you humor me?"

He laughed—a hearty Chamber of Commerce mixer laugh. "And a charming lady lawyer, too. You're dangerous."

"'I'm not bad,'" I quoted Jessica Rabbit. "'I'm just drawn that way.'"

Garland laughed again. I was getting good at this.

"Oh, dear," he said, still chuckling. "Charming and funny. You're lethal." He composed himself. "Well, how can I help you today?"

His manner was light and casual, but his voice had a purposeful undertone. Garland was no fool.

"I was hoping to talk to Darrell Cooper, but he's left Kozmik. I understand he moved to Philadelphia. I've been having a heck of a time finding him." I paused to let it sink in. "I hope you can provide a lead." I skipped over the part about Darrell being dead.

150

"Interesting." Long pause. I wondered if Garland knew about Darrell. Had I said the wrong thing? Maybe he'd hung up. "What makes you think I would know where he is?"

Garland may not have been a fool, but he was no expert at this game. An answer like that was too guarded, too cagey. I had the distinct feeling that he knew more about Darrell than he was telling. Smelling blood, I shoved my crib notes aside.

"As the vice president responsible for this subsidiary, I assumed you might be aware of the fact that Cooper left Kozmik shortly after the, uh, situation there arose." I avoided the term "embezzlement," because it reeked of legalese. "When I heard he went to Philadelphia, I thought, perhaps, he might approach you about a new job or a reference." I paused, sighing for dramatic effect. In my best forlorn voice, I said, "I don't know. I was just taking a shot."

Another silence. Please, please, I thought. Throw me a crumb.

"Cooper did call me recently, but not about a job or a reference. And I'm afraid I don't know where he is."

"What was it—?"

"Now, that's all I'm at liberty to say." Garland was all business now. "If you have any other questions, you'll have to direct them to our legal department."

Ah, the legal department. That pretty much said it all. "Okay," I said, working to keep my voice even and somber. "Thanks."

"Certainly."

I hung up, clapped my hands and said, "Yes!" The conversation had been short and Garland never gave me anything. But I would have bet my next retainer check that Cooper had gone to Philadelphia to use the contents of his lock box to rat out the Kozmik embezzlers. And, with any luck, those papers could clear Brad and point to the culprits.

φφφ

The next day, I had a lengthy conversation with the asshole attorney about the discovery dispute in the Divorce from Hell. In my experience, the term applied to all litigious divorces. I told him I wouldn't withdraw my motion to compel until he'd provided better answers. He said he had nothing more. Stalemate, putting it squarely in the judge's hands. The judge wouldn't like having to spend time listening to us argue. Judges always prefer that attorneys work things out. And my client wouldn't like it, because he'd have to pay for my time. I was running through his money quicker than a shoe freak at a Manolo Blahnik store.

I left the office and picked up the photos of our suspect, then drove to CID to leave one with the homicide detective on the Sondra Jones murder. At the front desk I was referred to Detective James Willard. He wasn't in. I remembered Willard from a case I'd handled as a public defender. He was the stoic, cynical type. Walt and I would have difficulty convincing him to shift his investigation from Brad—with a possible motive and the murder weapon— to someone doing business with Kozmik, who may have been in the wrong place at the wrong time.

I gave the desk sergeant my card with a note asking Willard to call me. As I turned to leave, I saw another familiar face—Detective Martin Derry, whom I'd dealt with on several occasions, not always happy. His navy suit enhanced his blue eyes. He stopped beside me.

"Do we have business?" he asked.

"No. I'm here about one of Detective Willard's cases." Despite the tension between us, I felt regret. He, on the other hand, looked relieved.

I'd last seen Derry several months before on a case in which he'd had to placate an FBI agent while investigating a homicide. Because it also involved identity theft, federal agents from an alphabet soup of agencies ended up crawling like flies all over the matter. Derry and I were hardly pals. Nonetheless, he ended up as the "good cop" to the FBI's "bad."

My problems with Derry began when I worked as a public defender. I'd won an acquittal for a man accused of killing his fiancée because the evidence against him had been mishandled. Sometimes I wondered if we would ever reach a truce. And even though it happened years ago, I knew that time doesn't always heal wounds.

"Anything interesting?" he said, drawing me back to the present.

"The Sondra Jones murder."

"Oh, yeah." Derry's chin dipped in a semi-nod. "The White Collar Killing. I thought Walt Shapiro was representing the perp."

"*Alleged* perp," I said. His jaw clenched. "The case has acquired a nickname, huh?"

"Let's just say it's not representative of our caseload." He meant drug killings, domestic disputes, gang killings—most of them involving minorities.

"Well, you may have to change the name, if the evidence I have for Willard turns up any other leads." I waved the tape before him. "The surveillance camera showed someone who did business with the suspect's employer coming and leaving ten or fifteen minutes before our client arrived. This guy." I held up the photo.

Derry did a double-take and squinted at the image. "Looks familiar. May I?" He took the photo and examined it.

"Do you watch old movies? He could've played a thug in a Forties gangster flick."

One corner of Derry's mouth upturned in a half smile. Shaking his head, he said, "Somewhere else." He looked at me. "I can pass this along to Willard."

I had hoped to deliver the photo to Willard myself. In the spirit of détente, I let him have it. "I'll let you, on one condition. When you figure it out, you agree to tell me who it is and where you've seen him."

His mouth pursed and his mustache curled over his bottom lip. "You know I can't promise that. It's not even my case."

Trying not to appear desperate, I looked him in the eye. "Please." *Groveling to a cop. Jesus!*

Sighing, he said, "I'll see what I can do."

On the way back to the office, I resolved to set up a time to see Tina. We were overdue for a talk about Rochelle's gang and the kid who'd been at her house around the time of the murder. No doubt, she felt abandoned and scared in detention. I wanted to tell her I was doing everything I could to get her sprung, without raising her hopes.

On the phone, I was bounced around to various people, until being handed off to the superintendent.

"Ms. McRae, I understand you wish to visit your client, Tina Jackson?"

"That's right." Something was wrong. They wouldn't route me to the woman in charge to arrange a simple visit. I remembered Tina's description of girls with toothbrush shivs. Fear gripped me. "Is she all right?"

"This is . . . difficult for me . . . ."

"What's happened?" I said, my voice rising with my anxiety.

"Tina . . . has escaped."

CHAPTER TWENTY

The superintendent didn't mince words: Tina had escaped with another girl. End of story. *Shit. Where the hell could she be?*

I felt a mix of relief, that Tina was no longer locked up, and fear about her roaming a dangerous world alone. If I found her, I'd have to turn her in. The thought made me sick. To defend her, I had to talk to her. First, I had to find her.

Little D had left a message for me while I was on the phone. I called back immediately.

"Tina's escaped the Patuxent Detention Center," I said. "Do you think she'll go to her father's?"

"Mmm," he hummed. It sounded like low C on a pipe organ. "It's possible."

"Can you nose around Fisher's? See if she shows up there? Or tell me if you hear anything on the street? I'm very worried."

"Me, too. But try to stay calm. She's pretty good at lookin' after herself."

Pretty good isn't enough, I thought.

"I called to remind you about tomorrow," he said. "Calvert Road Park. Half past noon."

"How'd the Iverson meet go?"

He chuckled. "Jus' fine. I got a pitcher of ole' Blue Jumpsuit givin' the package to Narsh. We followed the dude in the jumpsuit to Silver Hill Intermediate School. Found out later he's a janitor there."

"Tina's school."

"Yeah. So?"

"I don't know. Just another odd coincidence." The kind I don't believe in.

"And there's something else you ought to know."

"What now?"

I must have sounded worse than I felt. Little D just laughed and said, "No, this is good. After we followed the janitor, I convinced Narsh to let me make a couple copies of the disc in the package."

"Really? How'd you manage that?"

"I figured he wouldn't want Fisher to know how I out bad-assed his bad ass. Wouldn't want me to tell Fisher what we got and how we got it. He wasn't too happy, but he went along."

"So what's on the disc?" I asked.

"Haven't checked yet, but I'll let you know. Apparently, it's images, not data, on a DVD. You want to get together sometime, have a look?"

"How about you come over my place tomorrow, after the meet? Around five?"

I gave him directions before we hung up. Images. For computer games? Maybe the embezzlers were paying top dollar to steal a competitor's game concepts. If so, how did the janitor get them?

If it hadn't been for Little D, I wouldn't have known any of this. I felt grateful for his help. And I saw what Duvall meant about D's methods. They got results, but they were risky. It occurred to me that befriending a guy like Little D was like owning a pet scorpion.

φφφ

Saturday was a light-traffic day on the B-W Parkway. I got to
Riverdale with ease. Twenty minutes before the appointed
time, I pulled into the lot of Calvert Road Park, barely a
quarter mile from Kozmik's offices. I backed into a space
and flipped through last month's Maryland Bar Journal.

The October weather had taken an abrupt turn toward
winter. Clouds scudded across the sky, plunging the
landscape into patches of shadow and light. I counted a few
cars but saw no sign of life. I assumed people were out
hiking or biking the trails. The breeze kicked up, causing dry
brown leaves to spring to life and rattle across the lot.
Cracking the window for air, I sneezed. Leaf mold and the
smoke from burning firewood tickled my nostrils.

At 12:20, Narsh pulled into the lot in a beat-up maroon
compact. If he saw me, he never let on. I slumped in the seat.
He backed into a spot across and a couple of spaces down
from me. Loud rap music thumped from the car.

Five minutes later, a late model Saturn, light-blue, crept
up beside Narsh's car, drivers' sides facing each other like
cop cars. I saw the Saturn's window roll down and caught a
glimpse of a doughy-faced guy with glasses. Narsh and he
had a short, intense conversation, after which Narsh handed
him a brown envelope. My view was somewhat obstructed,
but I snapped a few pictures with my digital camera before
the Saturn's window closed.

Narsh left. As the Saturn backed out, I started my car. By
the time the Saturn had turned onto Paint Branch, I was
rolling. I followed the Saturn as he made a left at Kenilworth
Avenue, reaching the intersection as the light turned yellow.
Maintaining a distance of several car lengths between us, I
followed the car up the ramp at the Greenbelt Road
interchange and took a left, toward Beltway Plaza Mall.

The Saturn hung a right onto Cherrywood Lane and turned into a parking lot in the Spring Hill Lake apartment complex. I knew it well, having lived there as a student at the University of Maryland.

The car pulled into a spot. I kept an eye on it and cruised slowly past the lot's entrance. Two guys got out—the driver, short and soft-looking, with long brown hair and black-rimmed glasses, and the passenger, tall and gaunt, with curly red hair and pale skin.

I pulled over, snapped a couple of shots and noted the building they entered. While waiting to see if anything else went down, I checked my office voice mail. Detective Willard had left a message. I called him.

"Yes, Ms. McRae," he said, in his characteristic low rumble. "Detective Derry showed me that photo. I understand the man appears somewhere on the surveillance tape. Is that right?"

"That's right," I said. I told him what times Blondie had appeared on the tape. I also gave Willard a brief rundown on everything, including the hulk's previous visits to Kozmik Games, the trip to Philadelphia to see Cooper and Cooper's demise. As I spoke, I kept an eye on the building, in case one or both men decided to leave.

"Detective Derry mentioned to me that the man looked familiar," I said. "Did he ever figure out who it was?"

"Yes, he did. Don Diezman. They called him 'Diesel' Don or just 'Diesel', when he played fullback for the Terps in the late '80s. Was on the All-Met team in 1986. Had a shot at the pros, but he blew it by testing positive for steroids and getting busted for crack."

Serves me right for not following college football, I thought. "Well, I wouldn't want to be on the defensive line when he came through."

"You might want to avoid him off the football field, if he has anything to do with Ms. Jones's murder."

φφφ

I waited around, but neither of the guys came out, and I didn't recognize anyone going in. If one left, I could follow him home. For all I knew, they could be roommates. Surveillance sucks. After about an hour, I had to piss like a Pimlico contender. When it looked like they weren't going anywhere, I threw in the towel.

On the way home, I stopped for a bathroom break and picked up groceries. It was nearly quarter of five by the time I arrived at my apartment. There was a note on my door from FedEx, telling me I'd missed a delivery I had to sign for.

"Shit!" I said, stamping my foot. In all the excitement over the surveillance, I'd forgotten about the package from Alex Kramer. The note said there would be an attempt to redeliver on Monday. I groaned. Now I had to wait two more days to learn what Cooper had kept in that box.

When I walked in, I didn't see Oscar. Usually he waited for me at the door, begging for dinner. As I lugged the bags into the kitchen, I spotted him crouching atop one of the cabinets.

"What're you doing up there?" I asked, setting the bags on the floor and my purse on the counter.

"Staying outta my way, chickie-poo."

I whirled around. There stood Blondie—aka Diesel Don. He peered at me, his face devoid of emotion. He stood at the entrance to the kitchen, blocking the path to the front door like the Berlin Wall.

When I'd found my voice, I asked, "How . . . how did you get in here?"

"Locks in these apartments are a goddamned joke, you know." His tone was matter-of-fact, as if he were talking about the weather. "You really should ask the management for something better."

I nodded, feeling stupid. He just looked at me. "We need to have a little talk. See, you've been asking too many questions. My employers get nervous when people do that."

"Who employs you? I'll try to stay out of their way."

The hand came out of nowhere and slapped my head sideways. Then two hands shoved me back against the stove.

"Now that makes two things I don't like about you," he said. "You ask too many questions and you got a smart mouth."

"I have to ask questions," I gasped. "It's part of my job."

"And it's part of my job to take care of people who ask too many questions." He got in my face and glared at me with eyes as steely and lifeless as ball bearings. "So where does that leave us, chickie-poo?"

"Not in a real warm, fuzzy place, huh?"

My attempt to lighten the mood failed miserably. He took another swing at my face, connecting harder this time. My cheek tingled with the shock of his blow. I tasted blood which tickled my chin as it dribbled from the corner of my mouth.

He pressed me against the stove. With his face an inch from mine, he whispered, "Cooper's landlady told me you were in his room. Why don't you save me the trouble of searching your little shithole apartment and tell me what you found there."

"Just some papers," I whispered.

"Nothing else? You're sure?"

I nodded. I thought about the package I hadn't received. Did it have what he was looking for?

"Wasn't there a key with those papers?"

"What if there was?"

"Any idea what that key went to?"

"How would I know?"

He gritted his teeth in a menacing grin. "Anyone ever tell you you have an annoying habit of answering a question with another question?"

"Really?" I said, flinching when I realized I'd inadvertently done it again.

He grabbed my chin with one huge hand and squeezed, forcing me to look him in the eye.

"So you wouldn't have any photographs or recordings from Cooper?"

"What would I be doing with those?"

He pressed harder. "Answer the goddamn question, counselor. Yes or no?"

"No."

It was the truth, but his eyes narrowed and he said, "You're lying."

"I'm not," I sputtered. "I really don't have anything like that." *Though I might have, if I'd been here earlier to sign for the package* . . . .

He stared at me for a long moment. "Maybe you do, maybe you don't."

He wrenched one of my arms behind my back, pinning it between me and the stove. The other, he held at the wrist. With his free hand, he flicked on a burner. "We'll soon see how much you'll tell."

He started to push my hand toward the flame. I thrashed around, trying to free my legs enough to knee him in the balls, but he pressed me too tightly.

"Wait!" I cried in a desperate warble. "Okay, I know there was a key, but I don't know what it unlocked. And I don't have any photos or recordings. Don't believe me? You can search this place and my office, but you won't find them. Burning my hand won't change that."

He stopped, his gaze locked onto mine. "No, but it may teach you not to play with fire."

I squirmed some more, mining every ounce of strength to keep my hand from the flame. As we struggled, someone knocked on the door.

Little D, perhaps. I screamed at the top of my lungs.

Whoever it was began pounding the door as if thrusting a battering ram against it. Between my screeching and the pounding, Oscar freaked out. He launched himself from the cabinet onto Diesel's shoulder and dug his front claws into my attacker's face. Diesel howled and stumbled, tripping on Oscar's dish and flailing his arms. I leapt away from the stove and glimpsed Oscar streaking to safety as I fled the apartment. Passing Little D, who stood on the landing, cell phone pressed to his ear, I gasped, "He's inside," and ran downstairs.

Diesel barreled out of the apartment and hit Little D in the solar plexus, knocking the wind out of him. I looked up the stairwell and glimpsed Little D, lying in a heap as the killer lunged for the stairs. I ducked down the steps leading to the basement apartments and cowered. After Diesel left the building, I exhaled and emerged from the stairwell to find Little D recovering. He limped down the stairs and joined me on the ground floor landing in time to watch a black compact burning rubber out of the lot.

CHAPTER TWENTY-ONE

Little D didn't hang around for the cops. He said he and the police didn't "get along." He had dialed 911 because it seemed faster and easier than breaking down my door. I gave the police a report. When the patrol car left, I called D to give him the all clear.

He arrived fifteen minutes later, disc in hand.

"You all right?" he asked. "Damn, that's a nasty bruise on your cheek."

"I'll live." I felt lucky to have nothing worse than a bruised cheek and a puffy lip. "Thank God you came by."

He sat on my sofa. "That motherfucker strong. Rung my bell."

I explained what I'd learned from the police about Diesel.

"Hmm," Little D said. "I recall the name, but it's not one I've heard on the streets."

"Probably hangs out on different streets than you."

Little D chuckled. "Could be. So this Diesel all worried about some photos and shit in a box."

"That's what he was asking me about, while he was trying to barbecue my hand."

"Well, wait until you see this disc." He sounded disgusted. He gestured toward the tower of electronics next to my TV. "You got a DVD player in there somewhere?"

"Sure," I said. I grabbed the remote and turned on the TV and DVD player. I popped the disc in. Before closing the drawer, I said, "My guess is it's the prototype for some new video game. Is that what it looked like to you?"

"Just play the thing. I should warn you, what's on there ain't pretty. If it's for a video game, it's some sick shit."

I hit the button. The disc slid in and began to play. In a bedroom with stark walls, a young black girl went down on a light-skinned black man. Rap music played in the background. The girl looked to be Tina's age. Maybe younger. The man moaned as she worked on him.

"That there's the janitor, by the way," Little D said.

"Jesus," I said. I hit fast forward. The next scene involved the same girl and two other men. One entered her from behind, while the other got a blow job. Fast forward to another girl, stripping off her clothes, reciting a patter so filthy, a Marine would blush. A man watched her and jerked off. I recognized the other girl—Rochelle.

"Phew. Damn," Little D said. "This ain't no easier to watch the second time. Turn it off."

"Wait," I said. I continued to buzz through the sleaze featuring several men and a number of girls involved in lots of oral sex and stripping, a ménage a trois, and numerous ejaculations. Any attempt at a storyline was well buried. The dates and times in the corner showed me the scenes had been shot over several days in the last couple of months. The actors, if you could call them that, were all adolescent black girls and older black men. I locked onto a young girl sucking off a man as she fondled his balls.

"Tina," I said, with numb disbelief.

"Sheee-it," Little D said.

164

The scenes were so shocking, it didn't hit me at first: The date and time confirmed that Tina had done this last Wednesday night. The night Shanae was murdered.

I kept watching . . . couldn't tear myself away. A second scene with Tina, coupled with the first, established that from 6:00 to at least 7:36 Wednesday night she'd been busy working on a promising porn star career. No wonder she was late with homework assignments. Where was she later that evening? It was anyone's guess. I noted that Rochelle's last scene took place at 7:48.

Little D retrieved the disc. I shut everything off.

"Damn," I said. "Shanae was murdered between six and eight. A witness thinks she saw Tina leaving her house a little after eight. I can't even use her extracurricular activities to establish an alibi." I paused to reconsider what I'd said and slapped my forehead. "Or can I? I don't know where this was recorded. Maybe Tina didn't have time to get to her house before eight—a period of less than twenty-four minutes. That's when the witness saw a kid leave the house. I don't think this was recorded in Rochelle's room. Tina told me they were at Rochelle's all night."

"That didn't look like no teenaged girl's room to me," Little D said.

"Wherever they were, Tina was there until at least 7:36 and Rochelle until 7:48. Where was this place, and how did they get there?"

"Rochelle coulda driven her mama's car."

"She's only thirteen."

"You think that stop her?"

I nodded. "Good point. But Tanya—Rochelle's mother— had to go to the hospital that night. Her sister came by. She would've noticed if the car was gone, don't you think?"

"Then someone else drove them. Maybe one of those men. Maybe another girl."

"One thing's clear," I said. "I need to talk to Tina about what she and her so-called friends were up to that night. This appears to be her best—and only—hope of an alibi."

"Yeah, I'm sure she be happy to tell you all about it, too." The disgust in Little D's voice was obvious. "I really don't believe this shit."

I heaved a sigh. "We have to take this to the police."

"Those guys who picked up the package ain't gonna be too pleased about that."

"Neither will Diesel," I said. "Which is why we have to do it as soon as possible."

"Want me to make a copy for you first?" Little D waved the DVD around.

"That might be a good idea," I said. "In fact, make three. I have two cases this could affect, and I'll keep one for my files. I want you to hold onto all of them until I can take them to the police."

"Sure," he said. "You gonna be okay?"

"I'll be fine," I said, unconvinced.

φφφ

After Little D left, I made a list. Find Tina and find out her whereabouts that night. Get the copies of the DVD to the police. But first, I had to find another place to stay. I wouldn't sleep a wink in my apartment, knowing Diesel had broken in with such ease.

I glanced at my watch. My downstairs neighbor, Russell Burke, would still be up at 8:00. I took the stairs two at a time.

Russell answered the door wrapped in a royal blue velour robe, clutching his evening drink. Bitsy, his Scottish terrier ('Scottish terror' as I like to call her) yapped at his feet.

"You might have noticed the, um, commotion a few hours ago."

"I was out earlier, having dinner with a friend." He peered at me. "What the hell happened to your face?"

I raised my hand to touch my cheek, recoiling at the pain shooting through my jaw and cursing myself for not covering the bruise with makeup. "I'm attracting some unwanted attention from the wrong people." I sighed. "A guy broke into my apartment and attacked me. If a friend hadn't come along, I'd be a lot worse off. It scared the shit out of me. I'm going to a motel for a few days. I want to make sure Oscar's out of harm's way. Could he stay with you while I'm gone?"

"Not again," he said, with exaggerated annoyance. Russell had once honored a last-minute request to look after Oscar, when I was running from the Mob in another case. "When are you going to learn to stay out of trouble?"

"Not in the next three days or so."

"Or so?" He raised an eyebrow. His head inclined to peer down his well-sculpted nose at me.

"I don't think it'll be more than two or three days. Really."

"I'll have to keep him in a room," he said, in a nasal drone. "Separate from Bitsy."

"Good idea," I said. "Oscar has claws. He might mistake Bitsy for one of his toys."

"Ha ha ha." With each "ha," I could smell the Scotch on Russell's breath.

"One other thing," I said.

"There's more?"

"I don't know if I'll be back by Monday, and I'm expecting a FedEx that requires a signature. If I give you my spare key, would you sit in my place and sign for the package? It's due between eight and three o'clock. I'd leave a note on the door, but I'd rather not advertise that I'm away."

"Lord! Let me check my busy social calendar."

Debbi Mack

"I wouldn't ask if it weren't extremely important. Please, Russell."

He heaved a great sigh. "All right. I have nowhere to go. I can hang out in your place as easily as I can in mine."

"Thanks, so much. This means a lot—to me and Oscar. I'll take you to dinner when I get back. A small token of my appreciation."

"You're on. And don't worry about Oscar. I'll keep an eye on the little bastard as long you need me to." He touched my arm and looked into my eyes. "For God's sake, be careful."

"I'll do my best."

I ran upstairs to get Oscar and the spare key. I tossed some clothes and toiletries into an old gym bag—my version of luggage—and put in a quick call to Walt. He didn't answer, so I left a message, filling him in on the latest developments. I hoped his Saturday night was more fun than mine.

I had just finished camouflaging the bruise with concealer when the phone rang. A woman at the other end sounded breathless.

"Ms. McRae? This is Ruth Higgins. Walt's sister. He's in the hospital."

"Walt?" I went limp. "Oh, my God. What happened?"

"I found him on the living room floor. He'd been beaten to a pulp. The doctor says he's had a heart attack too. If I hadn't stopped by, who knows . . . . " I heard a sob at the other end. After a moment, she continued, anguish in her voice. "He's barely conscious, but he asked me to call and let you know. He said it was very important. He keeps mentioning a big man." At that point, she fell apart.

"I'm coming," I said. "Which hospital?"

168

φφφ

I raced to Laurel Regional Hospital, inquired at the front desk, and shot through a maze of halls to the CCU. Ruth, a short woman in her late fifties with a drawn expression and frizzy, bottle-red hair, looked as bad as she sounded. When I asked to see Walt, she told the nurse I was his niece. Five minutes, the nurse said, giving me her sternest look.

I crept into the room, rank with the odor of sickness and disinfectant. Walt was gray and immobile. Plastic tubes ran in and out of him. On one side of the bed, a machine monitored his vitals. His eyelids fluttered, and he extended a hand to me.

"Sam," he said, his voice raspy.

I walked up and took his hand in mine. "Walt. I'm so sorry." I choked up. Stifling tears, I bit my puffy lip, grateful that he hadn't noticed it.

"Nothing to be sorry about."

"That man. He broke into my apartment earlier today. I didn't think. I should have called you right away . . . ." The dam broke. Tears rolled down my cheeks. "If I'd called sooner, maybe you'd be okay."

"Don't be silly. Don't blame yourself." He squeezed my hand, then went on hoarsely. "Now listen. This scumbag is using me to get to you. Don't let him. Do whatever it takes to help my sister's boy."

"I will, Walt. You can count on me."

"I know I can." He gave me a weak grin. "Why do you think I brought you onto this case? I only work with the best, you know."

I returned the smile. "You're the best, Walt."

"Sure," he said. "But you're almost as good."

CHAPTER TWENTY-TWO

I stopped at the office to retrieve my active files, backup hard drive, and Rolodex, keeping a sharp eye out for Diesel Don or his black car. I set up my phone to forward calls to my cell. After borrowing an old laptop with a wireless Internet card from my friend, Jamila, I checked into a cheap motel on Route One and locked myself in my room, ready to do business on the run.

If only I could repaint my car, I thought glumly, while peeking at it through the curtains. Even at night, my grape-colored Mustang stood out like a purple beacon.

Staying at a motel gave me some peace of mind. Still, it seemed like the calm eye of a hurricane. One step outside, and I felt certain I'd be blown away.

I stayed in all day Sunday, organizing paperwork and my thoughts. I sat cross-legged on the bed, files fanned around me, and made another to-do list.

My first thought was to find Tina and wrestle the truth out of her. While turning her in would be unavoidable, I had to do it—to get the truth and protect her.

Second, follow up with the police about the child porn discs. They could be relevant to two murder investigations and evidence of a separate set of crimes.

Third, call Hirschbeck about the status of the audit and bug him again to check the computers for tampering.

Fourth, show Brad pictures of the guys who picked up the package and see if he recognized them.

Last, but certainly not least, figure out Diesel's part in this. I suspected his role was limited to hired muscle. I hoped that would be revealed after I got the package from Philadelphia.

Setting aside for the moment the question of how a couple of nerdy-looking guys hooked up with someone like Diesel, I focused on what I knew about the Kozmik Games murders. Diesel had been in Philadelphia, looking for Brad's old boss, Darrell Cooper. Soon after, Cooper was found dead in the water—suggesting that Diesel may have put him there. Making murders appear like accidents didn't jibe with Diesel's style, but that didn't rule him out as Cooper's killer.

Diesel was in Kozmik's office building around the time Brad's new boss, Sondra Jones, was shot. Knowing Diesel's proclivity for breaking and entering, Diesel probably broke into Brad's condo and planted the gun that murdered Jones. I hoped the cops could find Diesel and bring him in for questioning on that murder—preferably before he found me.

Meanwhile, I had a discovery dispute to work out in the messy divorce case, and a possible settlement in a simple personal injury matter. I was waiting for a hearing to be set on whether Tina would be tried as an adult. That issue might become moot if I could find her and get her to admit where she had been the night Shanae was murdered.

Once I'd made the list, I did triage. What first? The better question was, what *could* I do first? Right now, I couldn't reach Tina. If Little D could find her, I'd deal with her then. I needed Little D to give me copies of the disc before I went to the cops. Hirschbeck, I'd call the next day—get his Monday off to a good start. That left Brad. I phoned him, and we arranged to meet in the morning at his condo in Greenbelt to look at the photos.

That night, I tossed and turned, the next-door TV on until the wee hours. In my fitful, half-dozing state, I had nightmares. In one, Tina and I were running through Bed-Stuy, down filthy alleys, past drug dealers and prostitutes. It was dark. I was trying to get home, but the alleys and streets kept changing. I was lost and frantic. I dragged Tina by the hand. When I finally spotted my building, I realized she was gone. I felt torn between wanting to run for home and searching for her. My mother appeared out of nowhere in her bikini, smiling and laughing. I awoke with a start when a door slammed.

I sat up, heart racing, eyes darting around the room, in the pre-dawn light. The bedside clock glowed 6:35 in red. A door banged again. The door for the adjacent room.

I tried to relax, snuggled under the covers and closed my eyes. Another door slam. Then another. Some idiot, carrying luggage to the car, lacked the sense or consideration to prop the damn door open. By the time the commotion ceased, I was awake for good. I got up, grumbling.

Peeling off my night shirt and tossing it aside, I stumbled to the bathroom and took a hot shower, trying to wash away the memory of the bad dreams. I wiped a section of the fogged-up mirror and reassessed the damages to my face. My lip looked better. The purple spot on my cheek matched my car's exterior. Thank God for concealer. I combed my short auburn hair, threw on some clothes and called Hirschbeck. I left another voice mail then headed for Brad's.

On my way, I stopped at Greenway Shopping Center near Brad's development for a venti high-test brew at Starbucks. If it had been on the menu, I would've paid extra to have it administered intravenously.

I'd guzzled most of it by the time Brad ushered me into his place. A short hallway led to the living room, where an old sofa and a scarred wooden coffee table sat across from a gleaming high-def TV.

"Nice," I said, nodding at the TV.

"I bought it right before all hell broke loose. I thought I'd be able to pay it off quickly. Now . . . . " For a crazy moment, I wondered if Brad might be in on the embezzlement. Maybe he'd paid his co-worker Jon Fielding to mislead me. Christ, I thought. I'm really getting paranoid. No doubt, Brad liked expensive toys, like a lot of guys his age.

"You said you had some pictures to show me?" Brad asked.

"I do," I clicked through a few photos on my digital camera to shots of the two men. Brad squinted at the small screen and asked permission to download them to his computer, to enlarge the images. I watched over his shoulder as he plugged the camera into a port and performed technical magic that transferred the images to the hard drive.

As he opened one file, I asked, "Are you using Photoshop?"

"Uh-huh. My parents got it for me. A professional-quality program. Awesome for graphics and video, too."

I watched him fiddle with apps to enlarge and fine-tune the images. By changing the contrast and tint, he further defined the men's features.

Brad's jaw dropped. "Hey, I know them. They work for Kozmik." He became animated. "Chip Saltzman and Mike LaRue."

"What do they do for the company?"

"They're in game development."

Of course. The game developers who met with Diesel. "Are they computer programmers?" I asked, peering at the photos.

"One's a game designer, the other's a programmer."

Assuming the system was tampered with, who better to do it than a couple of computer geeks? "I think we've found our embezzlers," I said.

"You're kidding," he said, eyes wide. "What makes you say that?"

"I found a money trail, and it leads to them. Are they friends of yours?"

"Not like close friends." He looked away. "But I've gotten to know them. I never dreamed they'd do something like this to me."

"This must be a shock," I said. Brad nodded. He seemed unable to speak.

What I still didn't know was "why" and "how": Why were these guys using the embezzled money to buy kiddie porn? And how had a couple of middle-class white nerds gotten hooked up with a janitor from Suitland?

φφφ

When I left Brad's, my cell phone jangled. I flipped it open when I saw the caller ID.

"Hi, D," I said. "Anything new on Tina?"

"Naw," he said. "But I've got the janitor's name for you. It's Greg."

"Greg. That's it?"

"I find out more, I'll let you know."

"Okay. Where have you looked for Tina, by the way?"

"She ain't with dad and she ain't at her friend Rochelle's house, if that's what you were thinking."

"They'd both crossed my mind. Could she have gone home?"

Little D grunted. "Checked there too. No sign of her."

"I may run by and check again. I'm going to hit the school and pay a visit to Greg. If you're not busy, you want to sit in on our chat?"

"Wouldn't miss it," he said. "I'll bring your copies of the DVD with me."

"Great. I'll see you there."

"Ah-ight."

I thought about the DVD and all the questions I had for Janitor Greg. I hoped that, somewhere in his answers, there would be a solid alibi for Tina.

φφφ

Since I was in the neighborhood, I decided to run by Kozmik and get some face time with Hirschbeck. Enough with voice mails. I had to see him.

I approached the building and spotted Ana Lopez lighting a cigarette as she pushed through the front door. The same spiky-haired Ana Lopez who'd all but thrown me out of Kozmik's accounting department on my previous visit.

"Hi," I said.

She turned away, blowing a dragon's breath of smoke. "What do you want? Like I don't already know."

"I'm here to talk to Len Hirschbeck. I have some photos of the guys who may be the real embezzlers."

She cocked an eyebrow. "Really? Can I see them?"

Fascinating, her sudden curiosity. Might she be in on this? "I thought I wasn't supposed to talk to you about the case," I said. Ana rolled her eyes. Score ten for me. I snickered to myself for parroting her words. "For the moment, it would probably be best if I kept their identities confidential and shared them only with your legal counsel." I emphasized *only*.

She shrugged and struck another pose while taking a drag on her cigarette. "Whatever. How can you be sure you have the right guys?"

"I have evidence." I decided this would be a good time to test my theory that she had accused Brad of embezzlement. "Do you have any evidence to back your claim that Brad Higgins did it?"

Her jaw dropped. "I never. Who told you that?"

"Your whole attitude about Brad screams disdain for him. Tell me, is there solid evidence against him? Or did you accuse Brad because you wanted him gone?"

"I didn't," she sputtered.

"You accused him because you wanted his job, right? The job you thought you deserved."

Ana's mouth twitched. "Okay, look." She exhaled a ribbon of smoke. "*I* never accused him of anything. But I heard stuff about him. And he had this attitude. Like, he didn't need to worry because he would get his someday. He kept hinting he had it made financially." She took a drag and blew the smoke my way. "So when they found money in his file cabinet, I figured he was the one stealing. It would, like, explain his whole attitude, you know? And, yeah, it made me mad. I could have used that promotion and I never would have stolen from the company."

"Did it not occur to you that Brad's family may have money? That an inheritance would be his someday?"

She sniffed. A sapphire-blue stud twinkled in her nose. "Oh, really. Well poor, pitiful Brad."

"That doesn't justify accusing him of a crime."

"Look, all I said was he had this *attitude*." Ana dropped the cigarette and crushed it with her pointy-toed pump. "I never accused him of anything. I figured he did it, though."

I wasn't sure I bought her story, but I nodded and we went inside. As the elevator doors opened, she said, "I still think he's an asshole."

φφφ

Hirschbeck wasn't in his office and wasn't expected back all day. I hustled back to the car and sped off to Silver Hill Intermediate.

Little D was waiting in front of the school. I flashed my courthouse pass at the guard and explained that we needed to see Greg the janitor about a case involving one of the students. He took us to the administrative gatekeepers. After we'd received their blessing and our visitor's badges, the guard directed us to the custodian's office.

The head custodian was a stocky man with a shiny mahogany pate. Folds of fat collected above the back of his collar. "Greg's busy," he said, in a voice suggesting that he was, too. "Could you come back later?"

Little D stepped forward. "It's important we speak to him. Now."

The man's gaze traveled up the full length of Little D. "Well," he said. "I suppose I could page him, if it's that important."

Little D smiled. "We'd appreciate it so much."

The man walked to the nearby PA system and hit a button. "Greg Beaufort, please come to the custodian's office. Greg Beaufort, to my office."

He busily ignored us while D and I waited. The second Beaufort came into view, I recognized him from the video. He was short and slight, with close-cropped hair. His complexion reminded me of caramel candy. His crow's feet suggested he was in his mid to late thirties. He wore a dark-blue jumpsuit.

An adjoining room had a metal desk and a couple of chairs. I asked the custodian if we could use it. He grunted assent.

Walking in, Beaufort's glanced darted back and forth from Little D to me. "Whatchoo want?"

"I'm Sam McRae," I said, closing the door behind him. "I'm a lawyer." I paused to let it sink in. "I need to talk to you about something that affects my client. Have a seat, please."

His eyes narrowed, but he sat down. Little D leaned against the wall, arms folded, ankles crossed. I perched on a corner of the desk.

"First, I need you to verify how late Tina Jackson was at your place a week ago Wednesday. Second, I want to know how you got involved in the child porn business with Kozmik Games."

He glared at me. "Fuck you."

"We know Tina was at your place that night," Little D said. "We know about the sex parties." He stepped toward Beaufort, pulled a DVD envelope from his jacket pocket and waved it. "We have a copy of your, shall we say, greatest hits?" Little D's voice was calm, but the look he gave Beaufort could have melted steel.

Beaufort's expression changed. The cockiness vanished for a second. He collected himself. His temple pulsated. "Bullshit." He spat the word. "That could be Walt Disney you got."

"Fine. You don't have to believe us now." I shrugged. "After we give the DVD to the police, and they see Tina and her friends giving you and your buddies blow jobs, I think you'll start believing."

Beaufort's calm expression collapsed into panic. His eyes broadcast fear, his mouth trembled. He held his head. "Shit," he said.

"There's no point lying. Tell me how late she stayed that night."

"Shit," he said again. He covered his face, as if to wipe us out of his sight. "I'ma lose my job."

"You're going to lose more than that," I said. "Of course, if you cooperate, you might be able to make some kind of deal. You never know."

"For havin' sex wit' a minor? An' recording it, too?" He shook his head. "Shit."

Little D stood over Beaufort, staring down at him with growing disgust. At this last remark, I thought D might haul off and hit the little shitheel. I shook my head at him. D snorted. A wave of his hand said Beaufort was hopeless. D resumed his pose against the wall.

"Tell me, how late was Tina there?"

Beaufort held his face in his hands. "It was a little before nine when they lef'," he said.

"Are you sure of the time?" I asked.

"Yeah. They said their ride would be there at nine. They all come wit' some friend o' Rochelle."

I breathed a sigh. That was an hour after the neighbor thought she'd seen Tina leave her house. She had an alibi.

"So who was the friend?" I asked.

"I dunno." He saw the look on my face and his voice cracked. "Look, I really dunno. All I know is it was some friend, see?"

Little D looked at me, ready to have at him. I held him back with a raised hand. He scowled, but stayed where he was.

"So how did you get hooked up with the guys at Kozmik Games?"

"Say what? What guys?"

"The guys paying you for the porn."

"I dunno about no guys," he said, in a loud, exasperated voice.

"Well, why were you in Philadelphia looking for Cooper?"

I sucker-punched Beaufort with that question. His eyes widened and he stuttered. "Ph-Ph-Philadelphia? I ain't been there."

"Don't bother to deny it. There's a witness who can identify you." I didn't mention that the charming Elva McKutcheon thought all black people looked alike. For another twenty bucks she'd probably identify him—even if she didn't recognize him.

Beaufort squirmed. "I went there to find that dude Cooper, as a favor for a friend."

"What favor? What friend?"

"He wanted to talk to Cooper, is all."

"Who did?"

He shook his head.

"Someone with Kozmik Games?"

In one fluid motion, Little D sprang from his spot against the wall, grabbed Beaufort's arm and twisted it behind his back. "Start talkin', mutherfucker. And tell us the truth."

"I don't know whatchoo talkin' 'bout wit' 'dis Kozmik Game shit!" Beaufort was laying it on a bit thick, I thought. Either he really didn't know or he was lying at the top of his voice.

His rage barely suppressed, Little D glared at Greg. "You want me to break his arm?" he said quietly. Beaufort whimpered.

"That won't be necessary," I said, keeping a steady tone. "We have an alibi for Tina, either through him or the person who took Tina and the other girls home. Breaking his arm could be considered overkill."

"Too bad," Little D said. "I could stand a little overkill right now."

We left Beaufort sitting in the chair, head bowed.

φφφ

Little D had someplace to be. I decided to see Tina's guidance counselor before I left the building. I wanted to know if he'd heard anything more through the grapevine. Frank Powell's office was locked. One of the staff said he'd taken the day off. I made a mental note to call Powell the next day and asked to see the principal about the janitor's "after-school program."

The principal was tied up, but the vice principal agreed to see me. Reginald Thompson was bony and long-limbed, with a face as brown as a raisin and almost as wrinkled. His handshake and manner were firm and no-nonsense.

As I explained the situation, I watched his eyes display a kaleidoscope of emotions. His expression ran from disgust and anger over what Beaufort had done to dismay and anxiety over the fallout it would create for him and the school. When I finished, he sat staring into space for a full minute.

He pulled himself together and spoke in a controlled voice. "You know, I recall Tina's mother coming by, claiming one of our employees was involved in some shady business. I wasn't able to see her at the time. We knew she could be something of a loose cannon. Frankly, we didn't know whether to take her seriously. Maybe this was what she wanted to talk about."

My thoughts raced. Maybe Beaufort was another suspect in Shanae's murder, if he didn't appear on the DVD during the timeframe in which Shanae was killed. He even fit the description of the "kid" who the neighbor, Mrs. Mallory, saw leaving the house. Light-skinned and built like Tina—around her height and skinny. And he knew the girls were in a gang, so he could have beat up Shanae with the intent to set Tina up. Beaufort might be a viable suspect, if he'd been able to slip away unnoticed during the "festivities." But I wondered how Shanae had found out about the sex parties.

"Obviously, if this is true," Thompson continued, "we can't keep this man on. But I'll need proof before I can do anything."

"I can give you a copy of the DVD."

"I'll also want to talk to the girls involved in this mess. We will treat this as highly confidential, of course." He looked at me for confirmation.

"I have to take the disc to the police," I said. "It's evidence in other matters. You have my word that I don't intend to tell anyone else."

Looking glum, he nodded. I left one of my discs with him, figuring I could get more.

I got in my car and made the short drive to Tina's. The house was dark. No one answered my knock. Was the house empty? Or was I being ignored? I hoped someone had cleaned up the mess after Shanae was beaten to death. Finding the front door locked, I walked around back. Locked. A shade covered the window. I returned to the front and peered through a crack in the curtains. It was too dark to see.

I knocked at Mrs. Mallory's to ask if she'd seen Tina recently and struck out. Where was everybody?

Heading to the car, I noticed several black girls, standing around and watching me. I picked out Rochelle. They all wore pink—pink shirts or pink scarves in their hair or around one wrist. They walked toward me, Rochelle in the lead. I counted ten of them—and only one of me.

Her head bowed, Rochelle reminded me of a bull ready to charge. I stared into ten pairs of glaring eyes. I glanced at my watch. "I do believe you ladies are missing class."

Rochelle fixed me in her crosshairs. "I jus' talked to Greg. You leave him alone," she said in a low voice. "You hear me? And you leave Tina alone, too. She ain't going back to no juvie jail."

"Rochelle," I said, holding up my hands. "Wait a second."

"No, you wait a second," she snarled. She whipped a straight razor from inside her shirt and snapped it open. "You stay away from them, bitch, or I'll cut you up."

CHAPTER TWENTY-THREE

"Rochelle, listen," I said, as calmly as I could under the circumstances. "All I want is to help Tina."

"She was wit' me all night, okay?" she said, waving the razor in my line of sight. I kept it in view, prepared to duck if she lashed out. "Don't matter 'zactly where or what we was doing. She was wit' me."

I tried to swallow and could not. While my mouth was bone dry, my armpits were soaked. "I want to believe that, Rochelle. But the cops may think you're lying to protect her."

"I tole' you, I don't wanna be draggin' Greg into this."

"It's too late," I said. "I already spoke to Mr. Thompson about him."

"Sheee-it." She stopped waving the razor, but kept it raised. "Now I'ma have to deal with Mr. Tom, too? Thanks, bitch. You a real help."

"What Greg was doing is wrong. And it's illegal. Do you have any idea how serious it is?"

Rochelle looked at me like I was crazy. "So what about it?" She waved the razor, as she spoke. Every move sent shivers up my spine. "Ain't no thing. We had a sweet deal going wit' Greg. We was paid to do that shit."

So some of the embezzled money had trickled down to Rochelle and the gang. And I bet it was a trickle by the time it reached them.

"I'm sorry, Rochelle, but someone had to shut him down."

She gave an exaggerated shrug. "Fine. I guess we'll go back to selling drugs and stolen credit cards for money. It's riskier an' more work, but at leas' we won't be havin' sex," she said with mock horror.

Telling Rochelle that the gig was up seemed to defuse her anger. Maybe enough that she would answer some questions. "If you really want to help Tina," I said, "I could use some information. There was a tall, skinny kid here, around eight o'clock the night Tina's mother was killed. The neighbor thought it was Tina, but she was with you at the time. It might have been a boy. Or even a short adult. If it was a kid, I don't know what he or she was doing here." I paused. "This person could have killed Shanae. Or maybe came to see Tina and stumbled across Shanae's body." I stopped to catch my breath. "Is there anyone else you know who looks like Tina?"

Rochelle lowered the razor but kept a wary eye on me. "I dunno. Tina taller than mosta the girls, so she kinda stand out, you know?"

"What about a boy?"

"She don't have no boyfriend I know about."

"Do you remember if Greg stayed at the party the entire time you were there?"

"Yeah." She looked unsure for a moment, then nodded. "Yeah, he did."

Maybe it was true. Maybe she was lying to protect Beaufort. If only we all had foolproof bullshit meters.

"Rochelle, you and Tina and the others got a ride that night. I understand you left the party a little before nine. Is that so?"

Rochelle nodded.

"If the driver could tell the police what time you were picked up, it would provide Tina with an alibi."

"She can't."

"Why not?"

"She don't have no license. Jus' a car she borrowed."

Borrowed or stole, I thought. Scratch another alibi.

"In that case, Greg or someone else who was present will have to make a statement about the time you left Greg's place. I assume you were at Greg's."

"Yep."

"Whoever gives that statement will have to tell the cops all the details. That means, even if I didn't tell them, everything would still come out."

"Anyone can make a statement. They don't have to say what we was doin'."

"Rochelle, the DVD is evidence in another case. Apart from what these men did to you, I have to give it to the cops."

Rochelle gave me a blank stare. "DVD? Whatchoo talkin' 'bout?"

"Greg didn't tell you?" I paused to gather my thoughts. She looked at me like I was speaking Sanskrit. "Those parties were recorded. That's how I learned about this. And the recording provides airtight evidence that Tina was someplace other than at home, at least part of the night her mother was murdered. Getting someone to say exactly when she left is crucial."

Rochelle's eyes narrowed. A collective murmur rose from the gang.

"How much are they paying you to do it? The parties?" I asked.

Rochelle snapped the razor shut and slipped it into her bra. She turned to address her posse. "Y'all can go, okay." They dispersed. When they were outside of earshot, she spoke. "We need to talk bid'ness."

We both fell silent. The Branch Avenue traffic was a distant hum.

Rochelle fixed me in her gaze. "A hundred dollah a session. For me. The others get fitty. Way I see it, I set 'dis thing up, I should get more o' the cheese."

I shook my head. "Someone is paying thousands of dollars for these. They're doing something with those images, and they'll probably make much more than they're spending. And they're paying you shit." I paused for effect. "You're the talent. And they're screwing you in more ways than one."

Rochelle may not have given a rat's ass about statutory rape or child porn, but she sure understood money. She scowled, her eyes reduced to lizard-like slits. "Mutherfuckers. I din't know they was takin' pitchers."

φφφ

I got Rochelle's cell number and said I'd call her as soon as I was ready to go to the cops. Without pressure from me, she told me she'd heard from Tina but hadn't seen her since before her arrest. I told her she had to let me know if she heard from Tina. If we all went to the cops together, I hoped we could straighten things out.

I dismissed the thought of stopping at Russell's to see what was in the FedEx package before going to the police. I was too anxious to get the DVD into police hands, so I went straight to CID and asked for Detective Willard. A uniformed officer escorted me to Willard's desk.

"I wanted to give this to you," I said, handing him the disc. "I believe it's behind Sondra Jones's murder." I told him all about the DVD and the game developers who'd bought it from Narsh. I ran through my theory about the two of them stealing from Kozmik by hacking into the computer system to create the phony vendor account. I filled

188

him in on my surprise visit from Diesel plus my hunch that Cooper had been involved and had been silenced permanently because he knew too much. I told him that evidence I expected to receive later in the day might support the scenario.

Willard listened patiently, nodding and taking notes. He looked up. "Could you stop pacing, please? I'm getting motion sickness."

"Sorry." I didn't even know I was doing it.

"No problem. Go ahead and e-mail me the men's photos and names. I'll make sure someone looks into this as a separate matter, too." He waved the disc.

"Thanks," I said. "I'd like a copy to go to the detective on the Shanae Jackson murder. It shows my client was . . . otherwise occupied when the murder was committed."

He nodded. "I'll see that Detective Harris gets a copy."

Leaving the office, I felt great relief. I'd have good news for Walt. I hoped I could do the same for Tina.

As I walked out to my car, my cell phone rang. The number had been blocked, but I answered anyway.

"Ms. McRae? . . . Sam?" The voice faltered, but it was Tina's.

CHAPTER TWENTY-FOUR

My heart raced. "Tina! Where are you?"

"I . . . I'm all right. I jus' wanted to talk to you. What's going to happen to me?"

I didn't know, so I changed the subject. "Tina, we need to talk about the night your mother died," I said. "You were at a party that night, not at Rochelle's."

She paused long enough for me to know I'd taken her by surprise. "Who tole' you that?"

"It doesn't matter. The point is, you had an alibi, and you didn't say anything."

"But I was wit' Rochelle, jus' like I said. I jus' didn't wanna get my friends in trouble. I didn't wanna get Greg in trouble neither. This was their thing, and I didn't wanna stir nothin' up, you see what I'm sayin'?"

"You mean, it was part of the gang's thing and you didn't want to tell on them."

"Well . . . yeah."

We must be getting somewhere, I thought. At least she's no longer denying involvement in a gang. "Greg was recording you. That's how I know about all this."

"So what if he was?" she said.

"He was selling the recordings for big money and paying you girls peanuts to appear in them," I said. "He was using you."

"Ain't that what people do?"

Unfortunately, she was spot on, I thought.

"So what now?" she said.

"You need to come in," I said. "You and I need to go to the cops and make a statement about where you were, how late you were out, and all that. Greg Beaufort knows when you left. The cops will want to talk to him anyway, so he can verify your alibi."

"And then what? They'll jus' lock me up again, 'cause I run away."

"I don't know. Maybe we can work something out. But you can't keep running, Tina. You have to deal with it at some point."

"Deal with it? My moms is dead." Her voice turned steely. "She may not have been no good, but that's still some hard-ass shit to deal with."

"I know it is," I said. "Really, I do. My parents died when I was nine. It was . . . like they abandoned me." I hadn't verbalized that thought in many years. A headache gathered at the bridge of my nose, my eyes filled. I wasn't sure if I felt sorrier for myself or Tina.

"I'll be okay. I jus' wanted to see what was up wit' us. Don't worry 'bout me."

She hung up.

I cursed a blue streak that I hadn't gotten through to her. Tina didn't understand that she was hurting herself by avoiding the inevitable.

Suppressing my frustration, I headed for the nearest Starbucks with wi-fi. I fumbled my way through downloading the photos onto my laptop, e-mailed them to the cops, and made a few calls. Dancing Daria, my "bruised knee" client, had decided to accept the settlement offer. No more wasting time and compromising my professional reputation over her. After wrangling with Slippery Steve over the answers to my interrogatories in the divorce case, he promised to send me something "more complete."

"There's no such thing as 'more complete'," I told him. "Either your answers are complete or they aren't. I want complete. Nothing less."

"Ms. McRae," he said, in a practiced oratorical tone, "your argumentative skills remind me a bit too much of my ex-wife."

"Really?"

"Yes. That's why she's my ex-wife."

"Lucky her," I said, before snapping the phone shut.

Next I called Russell. He confirmed the FedEx package had arrived. I needed to take it off his hands soon. The last thing I wanted was to put Russell in harm's way. And I had to see what Diesel was so worried about.

φφφ

Russell brought the package to me at Starbucks. I accepted it with relief and trepidation. He bought coffee and joined me. Eyeing my healing bruise, he asked how I was holding up.

"Better now," I said. "If this package contains what I think it does. I can't thank you enough for your help, Russell."

"Well," he said, looking expectant. "Aren't you going to open it?"

"Not here." Anxious as I was, I didn't want to do it in public. My paranoia had kicked into high gear. I pictured Diesel marching through the door as I lifted the box top.

Russell looked baffled. "Would you tell me what the hell this is about?"

"I can't. Confidential case information. Anyway, you're better off not knowing, believe me."

He shook his head. "Why aren't you one of those lawyers who handles simple cases—wills or real estate closings or collections? How do you always manage to find trouble?"

"I don't. It finds me. And, if there's one thing I've learned after years of practicing law, it's that there's no such thing as a simple case."

φφφ

Much as I liked Russell, I was dying to find out what was in the package. We finished our coffee quickly, and I hurried back to the motel. Once I was safely locked in my room, I tore the package open.

Inside was a CD and several photos of Diesel with a man I didn't recognize. Scrawled on the back were the words: "Don Diezman with Max Fullbright" dated last April 26. Max Fullbright—never heard of him. On a hunch, I dug through Brad Higgins's file and found a copy of the Kozmik employee directory. Fullbright was listed as vice president for game development. Ha! I thought. This does go higher than the two computer geeks, Saltzman and LaRue. Another photo showed Diesel at a conference table with Fullbright and the geeks. On the back: their names and the same date. Co-ink-a-dink? Not likely.

I popped the CD into the laptop and turned up the audio. The sound quality was poor, but I could discern conversation about money transferred into an account earmarked for the development of a new video game. The money would pay for images to be used in a new interactive adult entertainment video. One man—probably Fullbright, I surmised, from his authoritative tone—said it was essential that this video game only be sold as discs and not be available online because of "possible federal complications."

Among all the euphemisms and cautionary language bandied about, I heard Diesel's unmistakable voice. "And what's my cut for providing protection for your little . . . enterprise?"

Fullbright offered ten grand, flat fee. Diesel made a harsh noise—laughing or coughing, perhaps. "You'll have to do a lot better than that, office boy," he said. He wanted a percentage of the profits. A back-and-forth ensued. I shut it off. I didn't care what they'd settled on. I'd heard enough.

Fullbright and his two-man crew must have decided to invest some of the embezzled money into a side project—an interactive child porn game, in which Rochelle and her gang were the stars. Through computer manipulation, the geeks would take those images and play with them, programming them to respond to user inputs. With the attention online child porn was getting at all levels of law enforcement, it was small wonder the game would be kept off the Internet, sold only as discs, and probably distributed in the same manner as illegal drugs—by word-of-mouth and under-the-table transactions.

As for Cooper, he must have found out about the embezzlement after Marzetti alerted him to the strange vendor account. I also assumed Cooper was paid to keep it hush-hush. Since this idea didn't surface for several months, he'd probably sensed the deal was headed in a direction he didn't like. He took the photos and recorded the conversation on the sly, in case he needed them as bargaining chips—either to keep his job, stay out of prison, or both.

I called Detective Willard at CID. He'd gone off-duty until the following morning. A clerk refused to give me Willard's cell number and put me through to voice mail. After a bad night's sleep and an exhausting day, I was ready to collapse. In my message I said I'd e-mail him more evidence related to the Jones murder in the morning. One more night in the motel, I thought. Tomorrow, it's off to Staples to copy the CD and the photos. I would then take them straight to the cops, before Diesel ran into—or over—me again.

CHAPTER TWENTY-FIVE

That night, I crashed like Sleeping Beauty on sedatives. Someone must have been watching over me. The adjoining room remained empty, and I awoke to my alarm instead of a slamming door.

I took a quick shower, cut short by my cell phone ringing. I couldn't get to it in time and toweled off before retrieving the message from Leonard Hirschbeck. "Please give me a call."

I combed my hair, put on jeans and a long-sleeved shirt, dabbed makeup on my bruise (a lovely mottled brown), and then called Tina's guidance counselor, Frank Powell. He was in the weeds—work had backed up and he had a full day of meetings. But he promised to be available at four.

Then I called Hirschbeck. Sounding resigned, he said, "The company approved the audit the day after we spoke. We paid extra for the auditors to work through the weekend."

"Considering someone's life is at stake, that seems fair," I said.

He ignored my sarcasm. "It looks like your client may be in the clear, if an expert can verify that the account information was altered. There was only one suspicious account. Which means someone deleted the account Marzetti found, or there was only one all along and someone tinkered with it to implicate Brad."

"I think that someone could be Max Fullbright, Chip Saltzman or Mike LaRue."

A moment of silence passed. Not surprising. I'd pulled those names out like rabbits from a hat. "Why?" he said.

"I have evidence that they're involved in the embezzlement. And a lot of other things the cops will want to follow up on. It seems they were using the money to develop a little project on the side." I summarized what I'd learned from Narsh, my surveillance of the two Kozmik employees, the DVD, and the contents of Cooper's lock box.

"Sweet Jesus," Hirschbeck said. He sounded appropriately shocked, as if discovering that his mother had been raped. "That's unbelievable."

"Since Saltzman is a programmer and appears to have had his boss's blessing, I suggest focusing on his computer. He may have used it to access the accounting files. And possibly to work on their after-hours project. If the lead pans out, you'll save a little time and money."

"Thanks," he said. He sounded dazed. "I want you to know that I meant it when I said I'm not the same person you knew in law school. I'm . . . sorry if we got off to a shitty start on this."

"You were trying to protect your client," I said, not wanting to rub it in or say "I told you so."

"I can't believe that about Fullbright." After a moment of silence, he added, "It's hard to know sometimes. Impossible, really. What people in your organization have been doing. You can't always know everything . . . ."

In other words, all clients lie. Ain't it the truth, I thought.

φφφ

No sooner had I closed the phone than it rang again. To my surprise, it was Marzetti.

"I need to talk to you." His voice was an anxious whine. "Can you meet me in Ellicott City in an hour?"

"I don't know, Vince. I'm very busy." I didn't need anything from him, and his previous stonewalling and hostility hadn't endeared him to me. Let him rot, I thought.

"I'll pay you for your time," he blurted. "There's something I have to tell you."

"Ookay," I said grudgingly. "Give me two hours. There's a matter I have to take care of first."

φφφ

I called Walt with the good news about the audit and that Brad was probably in the clear. He sounded tired, but relieved. I promised to visit him soon. In record time I packed my bag, grabbed my suit, checked out, and drove to Staples. The clerk copied everything, digitized the photos and put it all on a disc. Ah, the wonders of technology.

At Starbucks, I got online and e-mailed the audio file and photos to Detective Willard, explaining how I got them and what I thought they signified. I asked him to send copies to Detective Harris for her file on Shanae's murder.

With that out of the way, I drove north to meet Marzetti in Ellicott City, a historic small town whose Main Street curves up a steep hill, the road lined with rocky protrusions reminiscent of western Pennsylvania. By the time I parked, I was twenty minutes late. I raced to the coffee shop, arriving breathless. Marzetti was hunched over a small table in the corner. When he saw me, he jumped to his feet and nearly knocked over the table. He was jittery and without the bravado of our earlier meeting. We shook hands and I ordered coffee at the counter.

He started spouting before I sat down. "I know nothing about that account, okay? It showed up in the system, and I had no idea how. That's all I told Cooper. He was supposed to handle it from there."

I nodded and let him talk. Maybe I could learn more.

"A few months after I left the company, something odd happened. Cooper asked to meet me for a drink. I was surprised to hear from him. His call came out of the blue. He said he had a business proposition for me."

He leaned forward and raked his hair back with clawed fingers. "He brought someone with him." He stared at me, his eyes wide. "A huge blond man. Looked like a wrestler or a football player."

"What happened? What did he say?"

"The business proposition was a crock. He had no intention of proposing anything. He asked if I remembered the odd account I'd found before I left Kozmik. I said, yeah, I remembered. Cooper gripped my arm. It made me nervous. He told me to never mention that account to anyone, ever."

"Did he threaten you?"

"Not really. He seemed scared. And the whole time, the blond man sat like a statue, listening and staring at me. Like he was memorizing my features. Now and then, Cooper would pause or stumble over a word, and the guy gave him a look . . . ." Marzetti trembled. "A look that would freeze water."

I nodded. "Go on."

"Anyway, the last time you called me, you mentioned a large, blond man. I could never forget that guy. He freaked me out. Like when you came by my house asking all those questions. I'm sorry about that."

"No harm done," I said. "What changed your mind about talking to me?"

"On Friday, someone called me and said he was doing an audit for Kozmik Games. He wanted to know if I'd reported a suspicious account in the system. I said I didn't know what he was talking about. But now I'm worried." Our eyes met. He looked like a drowning man grasping for a lifeline. "Am I doing something illegal by not cooperating with the audit? Could I get into trouble?"

"I don't know. Your cooperation may not be necessary. Without going into details, I'll tell you this. It looks like they're going to check the system for tampering. So unless there's something about the account you're not telling . . . ."

"No. Like I said, one day it was there, and I had no idea how it got there. I told Cooper. When I asked him about it later, he seemed pissed off. He said, 'I wouldn't worry about it if I were you.' He was a moody guy. I didn't give it much thought until later when he told me to keep quiet." He glanced at his watch. "I should get back to work. So, you think I'm okay, not saying anything?"

I shrugged, unsure how to answer. "Why don't you let it be for now? If someone calls, you might want to share what little you know. If only to keep from looking like you're obstructing the investigation."

"Thank you, Ms. McRae," he said. When he reached for his wallet, I told him to put it away. I already had two clients involved in this mess. That was enough. He smiled and thanked me, and then he left.

I returned to my car and headed south toward the hospital in Laurel. I owed Walt a visit before dropping my stuff at home and going to the office. Cooper may have been paid early on not to blow the whistle and then intimidated into keeping mum when Diesel entered the picture after money went toward creating the child porn game. As an accountant, Cooper added nothing to the scheme. His only value was in keeping quiet. Why didn't they kill him? Maybe because the computer nerds and their boss weren't killers; Diesel was. Perhaps Cooper gathered the evidence against the embezzlers and Diesel, so he'd have something to trade if the people he was protecting turned against him.

The unanswered question was how Diesel and Greg Beaufort had hooked up with Fullbright and the geeks from Kozmik. Was it through Tina's father, Rodney Fisher? Was he the middleman?

Heading down Route 29, my cell phone jangled. It had rung more in the last week than in the previous year. I pulled over to answer it. "I have good news and bad news," Little D said.

I sighed. "Bad news first, please."

"Tina's alibi, Beaufort? He ain't talkin' no more."

"What's his problem?"

"His problem is he's dead. He hanged himself at home last night."

CHAPTER TWENTY-SIX

"Shit." I shifted the phone to my other ear. Who could blame Beaufort for killing himself? He had nothing to look forward to except prison and the stigma of a convicted statutory rapist and child pornographer. His death left me without a solid alibi for Tina.

"Now, the good news," Little D said. "I may have some witnesses who saw the girls leave Beaufort's place shortly before nine. If they saw Tina, they can back our story that she wasn't the one leaving her house around eight."

"They'd better be very observant witnesses," I said. "Eyewitnesses often remember things wrong. Unless they have a reason to remember her, it's likely they won't be able to verify that she was with the group. In which case, we're back to depending on Rochelle and her friends for Tina's alibi. I don't know how credible a friend's word will seem to the police. Especially friends like these."

"I can try to hunt down some other men at the party," Little D said. "The cops will want to find them anyway. Maybe one of the witnesses knows the men."

"That's a thought," I said. A tractor-trailer swept by, rocking the car. The shoulder of Route 29, a six-lane highway, was not the best place to chat. I wrapped it up quickly. "I wish I could talk to Tina. Any luck there?"

"Not yet," he said.

I reminded myself to call Tina's guidance counselor, Frank Powell. I asked Little D to keep in touch and said goodbye.

En route to the office, I considered what I would do if I couldn't find Tina. Should I bring Rochelle into this? Would her word alone be compelling enough to nip the matter in the bud? Or should I start exploring other options? And what about Fisher? There was still the possibility that he'd murdered Shanae after she threatened to reveal the source of his extra income. I needed to find out if he had an alibi for that night.

φφφ

I had a pleasant visit with Walt, dropped my stuff at home, and picked up Oscar at Russell's. I got to the office about 2:00 P.M. Sheila, the receptionist, eyed me suspiciously and asked where I'd been hiding.

I told her I'd taken yesterday off.

"You wouldn't believe how many people trooped in and out of here looking for you," the gray-haired receptionist rasped. "A courier left a package for you. Three clients dropped in to chat about their cases. And some blond guy who looked like Mr. America was hanging around. Wouldn't even tell me what it was about."

I felt the hairs rise on the back of my neck. I couldn't imagine what Diesel might have done to me during business hours. If his intent was to intimidate me, he had succeeded.

"When I told him you weren't here, he went upstairs to shove a note under your door," Sheila said. She handed me the package and a pile of mail. "Here you go. You're welcome. Next time, I'd appreciate a heads up when you go AWOL."

When I had picked up my files before checking in at the motel, I'd made sure to lock my office door. From the top of the stairs I could see that the door was shut, but not completely latched. Someone had jimmied the lock.

I opened the door a little at a time. The place had been turned upside down. The file drawers had been emptied. Files scattered about like confetti. The desk drawers were open, contents in disarray. My computer was on. The intruder hadn't been able to get past the security code I'd installed.

The intruder had been thorough. My framed diplomas and bar license lay on the floor, the backings sliced wide enough for a hand to check behind the certificates. My bar certificate had incurred a small cut. It was barely noticeable. My eyes fell on my father's photo of Jackie Robinson. It had received similar treatment. Gasping, I ran over to examine it. I was grateful to find it in good condition. Any nicks on that photo and I would have inflicted bodily harm on the perp.

I surveyed the wreckage, despairing at the prospect of putting everything back together again. No equipment was missing, but it was obvious someone had been looking for something. Did Diesel do all this while he was up here, pretending to leave me a note? It was possible as I had most of the top floor to myself. Maybe he'd used the opportunity to scope the place out, then returned later. He could have picked the front door locks so my landlord wouldn't notice the break-in. And once he got to my office, the contents were fair game.

If he'd done this, why hadn't he done the same to my apartment? Maybe I'd surprised him and come home before he'd had a chance.

I gathered papers and set them in piles. I would sort them out later. I checked to see if any of my visitors had actually left a note. An unfamiliar business card lay in the wreckage near the door. I picked it up. "Fisher's Pawn Shop, Rodney Fisher, Proprietor." On the back, someone had scribbled, "We need to talk, RF". I found no other note or envelope. It's unusual for a client to drop in without an appointment. If someone wanted to waste my time and their money, they usually did it by phone. I faced the possibility that someone other than Diesel had done this. One of my other so-called clients.

I sprinted downstairs. "Sheila, did anyone else go up to my office? Or leave anything with you?"

"Two of 'em left envelopes that I stuck with your mail," she said. "The blond guy and two others went up to your office."

"The ones who went upstairs. What did they look like?"

"One was a youngish, very dark-skinned black man. Kind of bulked up—you know, the sort with muscles on his muscles. Had his hair in those braids . . . ." She snapped her bony fingers in double-time. Sheila might have been twice my age, maybe more, but she had the manual dexterity of a twenty-year-old. "Whatta ya call 'em?"

"Cornrows," I said.

Sheila pointed at me. "Right."

That sounded like Narsh. He must have delivered Rodney's card.

"What about the other?"

She closed her eyes. "Another black man. He was short and skinny with light-brown skin. Wore sunglasses and a baseball cap."

The description fit Greg Beaufort. Clearly, he had tried to disguise his looks. "Were they together?"

She shook her head. "The darker fellow was here yesterday morning. The other guy came in the afternoon."

Greg Beaufort had likely been told to leave work after I'd talked to the vice principal. Had he come here to beg me not to report him to the cops? Did he break into my office to search for the DVD? If so, perhaps his failure to find me or the disc was the final straw for Beaufort. And he chose to kill himself rather than face the consequences. Maybe, I thought. It was all speculation.

I shook my head, dispelling possibilities and refocused on facts. "What about the blond man?" I asked. "When was he here?"

"This morning. Why do you ask?"

"Okay, don't freak out. But I think one of them broke into my office."

Her blue eyes widened. "You're joking. Is anything missing?"

"Nothing obvious. I'll have to look through the mess before I know for sure. The place got tossed. Whoever did it was looking for something related to two cases I'm working on." Since Narsh had left Fisher's card, I focused on the remaining two as possible suspects. Either could have had reason to break in and rummage around. "How long were those guys upstairs?"

Her brow furrowed. "The dark fellow with the corn rows might have been five minutes. As for the lighter-skinned guy, I can't say. I left my desk to help Milt organize his files. So I couldn't tell you exactly when he left."

"And the blond?"

"God, I don't know." She rubbed her forehead. "I wasn't paying close attention. And I had my earbuds in, transcribing letters. I couldn't hear a thing other than Milt, droning on about capital gains." She bit her lip.

"Don't sweat it," I said. "You didn't know there'd be a pop quiz."

"Okay." She sounded a bit shaky. "Are you going to call the police?"

I'd been so wrapped up in figuring out who and why, I had forgotten about the police. "Far as I can tell, nothing expensive has been stolen," I said. "But I'll call."

CHAPTER TWENTY-SEVEN

The police came and took my report. I had little faith that much would come of it since nothing big had been stolen. All my files were accounted for. I'd had my backup hard drive at the motel—out of sight and out of reach.

I placed a call to Little D. "Someone broke into my office," I said. "I think it was probably Beaufort or Diesel."

After I'd explained what Sheila had said, Little D said, "Well, it's too late to ask Beaufort and I don't think you want to ask Diesel."

"But I would like to talk to Fisher," I said. "He sent his little errand boy, Narsh, with an invite to see him. You doing anything this afternoon? I want to go by Fisher's shop and see what he wants."

"I can meet you there at three," Little D said.

"See you then."

φφφ

Little D was waiting for me when I pulled up in front of Fisher's Pawn, in a line of forlorn shops on Silver Hill Road.

We walked together toward the shop, wedged between Rayelle's House of Beauty and The Chicken Shack. The air reeked of hot grease and singed hair.

In the pawn shop, a transparent counter extended the length of the store, reminding me of a bowling lane. A Plexiglass wall separated the counter from the crammed-together merchandise. Everything from computer monitors to old radios and musical instruments packed the shelves.

A short, slight man, café au lait in color, looked up from the far end. I could see his resemblance to Tina.

"Rodney Fisher?" I asked.

"Who wants to know?" he asked, in a low, gruff voice.

"I'm Sam McRae." I held up his card. "You wanted to see me. And it so happens, I want to see you."

Fisher opened a gate and emerged from behind the counter. He strode down the long aisle toward us, eyes fixed on me. He seemed to be on a mission. I sensed Little D's presence behind me. My stomach felt hollow with anxiety.

Fisher stopped about ten feet away. His gaze bore into me. "Where is she?" he asked. "Where's my girl?"

I blinked. "I have no idea where Tina is. I was hoping you might know."

"How would I know? I ain't seen her. But you know, don't you?" He was looking past me now, at Little D.

"Mr. Fisher, I need to ask something else," I said. "Where were you a week ago Wednesday night—the night Shanae was murdered?"

"What bid'ness is that o' yours?"

I started to speak, stopping when I realized that, like Greg Beaufort, Fisher was skinny and short. And they were both light brown. He looked more like Tina than Greg had. In the right clothes, with a cap pulled low over his face, he could have passed for Tina. And he could have left the house that night—after killing Shanae.

"I'm interested, Mr. Fisher, because I know Shanae had evidence she wanted to use to get more child support." I chose my words carefully. "I know that must have worried you. And maybe made you mad at her."

"Yeah, bitch stole that shit from me. But so what? I di'nt have nothing to do wit' it. I was jus' the middleman, you know?"

Recalling the evidence Little D had shown me, I said, "She stole the financial records."

"Nah, not records. Some stuff wasn't even mine, you know."

This was news. Big news. I paused, trying to figure out what he meant without revealing that I didn't have a clue. "She stole that stuff. And she used it to force you to pay more money," I ventured, praying he'd fill in the blanks.

"Well, sure, then she got all pissed off when she find out what it was. But that shit not even mine. I dunno nuthin' 'bout that shit. I di'nt care, so long as I got my ten percent. You know what I'm sayin'?"

I got it. "She took one of the packages. One of the DVDs." She had found out about the janitor and the sex parties.

"Yeah. Whatchoo think I meant?" His glare shifted back to Little D. "Now, my man Narsh say you got Tina. So where is she, niggah?"

I turned to look at Little D, who had locked eyes with Tina's father. "D," I said. "Is this true?"

The front door flew open, banging against the wall. Startled, I yelped. Little D flinched and turned to face Tina's uncle, the portly William Jackson. The stink of booze rolled off him in waves.

"You knew," he bellowed at Fisher. "You knew what my niece was doing, but you didn't care. Her own father!"

Fisher's face contorted. "Whatchoo talkin' 'bout? You seen my Tina?"

"Yeah, I seen her." Jackson staggered toward Fisher. Little D and I stood between them. "She's safe, wit' me. I intend to take her far from you and your filthy bid'ness." He pointed at Little D. "He tole' me all about the shit she been doing so you can make a little money on the side!"

I gawked at Little D, but he looked away.

"But I dunno nuthin' 'bout that," Fisher whined. "I swear."

"Did you set it up with them white boys?" A drop of sweat etched a line down Jackson's cheek. "Did you set it up so my girl would be a ho' for them dirty videos?"

"I didn't set nuthin' up," Fisher muttered. "He came to me."

"Who?" I asked. "Beaufort? One of the white guys?"

"It weren't no white guy." Fisher shifted from foot to foot. "I dunno his name. He never said."

In seeming slow motion, Jackson reached into his jacket. Little D grabbed me and threw me against the wall, sheltering me with his body. I heard two shots. Fisher crumpled and fell. The door banged again, and Little D released me from his hold. For a moment, it was the three of us again—me, Little D and Fisher, a pool of blood spreading beneath him.

People emerged from nowhere, crowding inside, babbling. The air was pungent with cordite and the odor of lye-based hair straightener. Women from the beauty parlor—beauticians in pink aprons and ladies with damp, half-combed hair—screamed and swooned. Men mumbled and shook their heads.

"You see that mutherfucker run outta here?"

"Yeah, man, I saw him. He took off in that blue Mercedes—"

"Blue? Mutherfucker, that car was gray—"

"Whatever it was, he musta been doing ninety mile a hour."

I kept my eyes averted from Fisher and focused on Little D. He returned my gaze. Without a word, we picked our way through the swooning, mumbling crowd and stepped outside. Feeling woozy, the gunshots still ringing in my ears,

I took a moment to steady myself, before pulling out my cell phone and dialing 911.

As we waited for the police, Little D said, in a low voice, "You understand why, right?"

"Tell me, anyway." My voice sounded tinny and far away, obscured by the ocean roar in my head.

"Tina came to me, 'cause I was friends with her mom. If I'd turned her over to you, you'd have had to take her to the police. If I handed her over to her dad, they probably would've found her with him." He gazed at the traffic on Silver Hill Road. "I wanted to make sure we had an alibi for her, before that happened."

"So you left her with her uncle?"

"I knew him, figured she'd be safe with him." He shook his head. "And I knew he didn't like Fisher, but I didn't figure on him doing this."

I nodded. "I do understand. You did what you thought was best."

"And now, we standing out here with no more information than we had before."

"Maybe a little more," I said. "Maybe a little."

CHAPTER TWENTY-EIGHT

A long series of interviews ensued. They started on the scene and moved to a CID interview room when it became clear this was much more than a garden-variety shooting. By the time we arrived at the station, my ears were still ringing, but not enough to drown out the cops' persistent questions.

"And why were you at Fisher's Pawn?" the detective asked for the third time. A disheveled fellow in a shiny brown suit that matched his hair, he'd told me his name. For a million dollars I couldn't recall it.

"As I said, I was trying to locate my client, Tina Jackson. I thought Fisher might know where she was." I nodded at Detective Tamara Harris, a short, solid woman with freckled skin and a mini-Afro. Harris, the investigator on Shanae Jackson's murder, sat beside Brown Suit, tossing questions from time to time but mostly listening. On behalf of the State's Attorney's Office, my "good friend" Ray Mardovich was there. He wore the remnants of the bruise I'd inflicted. To my surprise, he also had a tape across his nose. I took guilty pleasure in having broken it. Ray sat next to Detective Harris, but I ignored him.

"Little did I know," I went on, "that Tina was with her uncle. What's going to happen to her, now that her father and Bill Jackson are in the hospital?"

"Don't worry," Harris said. "We're taking care of that."

Jackson had fled the scene, like a stock car racer on speed, only to wreck his car a few blocks away. He'd veered to avoid a pedestrian, bounced off another car and smashed into a telephone pole.

Harris spoke in rapid, no-nonsense bursts. "Fisher was a potential suspect from the start, but he had an alibi." Ray started to say something. Harris silenced him with a look. I began snickering and pretended to sneeze, to cover it.

"Given the way Shanae Jackson was killed," Harris continued, "we started looking at the gang angle. Girls usually don't use guns. They tend to go with bats or razor blades. Anyway, the forensics seemed to back our theories. When the neighbor placed a young girl who looked like Tina at the house around the time of the murder, we figured we probably had our killer. If it wasn't Tina, we thought it might be one of the gang. We hoped Tina would squeal on her."

"But Tina and her gang were busy that night," I said. "Detective Willard should have the DVD that shows what they were doing." I looked at the two-way mirror on the wall. Willard was no doubt watching.

"Yeah, I saw it. Even if Tina left before her friends did, I think the recording *probably* gives her an alibi. She was at Beaufort's place about twenty minutes before the witness thought she saw her at the house. That doesn't give her much time to go home and kill mom. So, we're left with the ten-million-dollar question: 'If she didn't do it, who did?'"

"I've been trying to figure that out," I said. "I think it may have been someone Shanae was blackmailing. Possibly the janitor, Greg Beaufort, though he would have had to sneak away from the party first. Fisher seems to be the more likely suspect. Both were short, light-skinned black men, but Fisher looks a lot like Tina. If he'd dressed in the right clothes, he could have passed for her."

"But Fisher had an alibi," Harris repeated.

"Right," I said. "Before he was shot, though, Fisher said someone had set up the arrangement between the boys at Kozmik Games and Greg Beaufort. I'd been wondering all along how these people got together. I think Fisher knew who it was. I know it wasn't a white man, but that's about all. Whoever it was would have been threatened by Shanae's knowledge of the setup."

While I was talking, Detective Willard walked in and leaned against the wall. A dark-haired white man in a navy blue suit stood by his side. "Ms. McRae, this is Detective Norris from Philadelphia," Willard said. "We've been touching base on Darrell Cooper's homicide and how it may relate to the Jones murder."

"Nice to meet you, Detective," I said. I was starting to feel like I'd walked into a cop convention. "So it was a homicide?"

"We have reason to believe so," Norris said. Apparently, he didn't want to talk about those reasons.

"The evidence you sent gave us grounds to bring in the two Kozmik game developers and their boss, Mr. Fullbright, and get a warrant to seize their computer equipment—at home and at work," Willard said. "They've lawyered up, but if we find child porn on their computers, there won't be much for them to say."

"How about the embezzlement?" I asked.

"They aren't talking, about the embezzlement or anything else," Willard said.

"I have copies of a check written on Kozmik's account to ITN, and financial records mentioning ITN that someone broke into Fisher's office to get."

"Since the police weren't involved, there's no Fourth Amendment problem with that. We'll need the person to testify how he got the records."

I tried, but failed to imagine Little D being a witness for the prosecution.

"I didn't get them," I said. "But I can tell you what I know."

"The question remains." Ray spoke at last, his voice nasal. "Who killed Shanae Jackson? More to the point, who can we *prove* killed her?" Harris nodded. I didn't have a ready response.

φφφ

Later, I sat in Frank Powell's office, still trying to make sense of everything I'd learned over the last few days. I asked Powell, rocking in his squealing chair, whether Beaufort had ever told him about the Pussy Posse's ventures into child porn.

Powell shook his head. "No, he never mentioned that. He did tell me the kids were having sex, but nothing specific."

"Would you have any idea how Beaufort might have hooked up with a couple of white guys at a computer gaming company?"

He spread his arms. "I haven't the slightest notion. I didn't know Beaufort well. He was a source of information. That's all."

"Hmm. Do you know if he knew a man named Darrell Cooper?"

He shrugged. "As I said, he was merely someone who kept me abreast of the school grapevine."

"Frank." A secretary stuck her head in. "Reggie says he needs to see you."

"I have a meeting here." Powell sounded annoyed.

"He says it's important."

Powell sighed. "My boss calls. I'm sorry. Will you excuse me a moment?"

"Of course."

Powell left. I got up and wandered over to examine his photos. They were mostly of football teams Powell had played on. I scanned the pictures and discovered that he was on the 1986 All-Met team. Goosebumps puckered my flesh. I'd heard of that team before. I checked the caption. There he was—Don "Diesel" Diezman, the fullback. In the next row was a name I hadn't expected to find—Darrell Cooper. He played center for the team. Powell was quarterback.

I looked at the jerseys. Diezman wore number 44. Powell wore 17. The numbers in Cooper's calendar.

CHAPTER TWENTY-NINE

I left Powell's office before he could come back and tell me more lies. I drove about a mile, pulled over, and called CID. The man who answered said Detective Harris wasn't in, and Detective Willard was in a meeting.

"I think I've solved one of Detective Harris's cases," I said. "At least, I'm reasonably certain that I have a prime suspect for her."

"Really." I heard a suppressed guffaw. Sure, Crimesolver Sam, doing police work now. Tell me another one, I expected him to say.

"The guy just lied to me about knowing someone connected to the case. Plus, he's in exactly the kind of position that would enable him to commit the crime." As Tina's guidance counselor, Powell must have arranged to meet Shanae at home, ostensibly to talk about Tina. She no doubt appreciated this accommodation since she hated going to Tina's school to discuss her problems. Shanae must have wanted to discuss Tina's performance with Beaufort on the DVDs. Powell had to know it was a matter of time before his part in the arrangement came out.

"So shall I have one of the detectives call you?" the man said, in a voice appropriate for dealing with small, unruly children.

"Can I have Detective Harris's cell phone?"

"I can take a message."

I gave him my cell number and told him to have her call right away.

I leaned back with my eyes shut. A sickening feeling overcame me. I shouldn't have left Powell's office. He would wonder about that. At some point, he would think of the photos and realize that they tipped me off to his lies. Which meant he'd come after me. Or he'd send Diesel.

I wondered if there was a motel far enough away for me to hide. And what would I do with Oscar? He didn't travel well. I couldn't ask Russell to take him again.

My phone rang. Reed Duvall's cheery voice greeted me.

"Hey," I said, trying to collect my thoughts. "How was your trip?"

"As good as it gets when you move your mother into assisted living," he said. "Now that's done and I've got a week's worth of backup to deal with. I thought I'd check in and see how things are going."

"Funny you should ask," I said, pondering how much had changed in a week. I gave him a bare bones update, including my revelation about Powell. "I'm trying to figure out where I can hide from a homicidal guidance counselor and a killer with a body that would make Arnold Schwarzenegger weep with envy."

"Let me help."

"Don't tell me. You'll give me your frequent flier miles to go to Tahiti?" The truth is, I've never been on a plane and I'm scared to death of flying, but I would ride shotgun with The Red Baron rather than face Diesel again.

"How about this?" Duvall said. "I'll be your bodyguard."

φφφ

"This is not the kind of service I usually provide," Duvall said, two hours later in my living room. "But, in your case, I'll make an exception."

Duvall had brought a small overnight bag that Oscar sniffed with great enthusiasm.

"I can't offer much in accommodations. I hope you don't mind sleeping on the sofa."

He grinned and brushed back the light-brown cowlick over his brow. "Of course not," he said. I thought I saw a glimmer in his green eyes. Unspoken desires?

"I can offer you dinner. I hope you like leftover moo goo gai pan."

"But what will you have?"

I shrugged. "I don't know. Bread and water, maybe?"

Duvall went to the kitchen and opened the frig. "You've got eggs. I see cheese and ham. I'll make us omelets."

"Duvall, you don't have to cook—"

"Shut up. Sit down. Let me handle this."

I sat at the breakfast bar, answering occasional questions about the location of my pans and bowls, and watched as Duvall made magic in the kitchen. While the eggs sizzled, he grated the cheese, shredded some deli ham, and retrieved a few slices of green pepper from the salad-in-a-bag I kept in the produce drawer. He diced them, added them to the other ingredients and folded the eggs over the filling. The place smelled heavenly.

As he toiled, I described the events of the past week and a half in greater detail, noting how much Little D had helped.

"He didn't tell me about Tina," I said. "But I understand his reasons."

"I told you he has his own way of doing things, didn't I?" Duvall said. "You can count on him, though, when things get rough."

As he slid the omelets onto plates, I said, "That stove will need a vacation. It's not used to working that hard."

"I should bodyguard you more often."

"Thanks for dinner. And thanks for coming over. I'm still feeling shaky."

"Don't worry," he said. He placed his hand on mine. I thought about moving it, but didn't. "I'm here for you."

I thought about Ray and the difficulties of getting involved with a business associate. His touch conveyed concern, maybe more. I told myself that Duvall and I should remain friends.

"But you can't look after me day and night," I said. "When the hell is that detective going to call?" I added, trying to change the subject.

"I'll do what I can. Maybe we can go to the cops tomorrow and insist on seeing someone. I know people there. I can pull some strings."

"I can't rely on you all the time to protect me and pull strings for me," I protested.

He looked at me. "Why? That's what friends are for."

Without thinking, I leaned forward and kissed him lightly on the cheek.

"What was that for?" he asked.

"For friendship," I said. "And a great omelet."

My phone rang. Detective Harris relieved us of the need to say anything further.

CHAPTER THIRTY

"We'll bring Powell in for questioning," Detective Harris said, after I explained what I'd seen in his office. "And get a warrant to seize those photos. We'll need a statement from you, too."

"Okay." I'd have to remember to bring in my copies of Cooper's calendar and the ITN invoices, which I still had stuffed in the file. "The question is, if I give a statement, will you have enough to hold him?"

"It seems likely. It's the most solid evidence we have of a connection between Powell, Cooper, and the child porn operation. It provides a strong motive for murder, if we can show Shanae Jackson knew about it." It was one big "if," and not the unqualified "yes" I was looking for. But it would have to do.

"Have you made any progress in finding Don Diezman?" I asked.

"Detective Willard is trying to track him down."

"How about Tina?"

Detective Harris drew a big sigh. "We're doing everything we can to find her. She wasn't at the motel where her uncle was staying."

My heart sank. Where could she be? "And her father? How's he doing?"

After a pause, she said, "I'm afraid he's dead."

The news hit me like a gut punch. With her parents dead and her uncle headed to the slammer for murder, what would happen to Tina?

φφφ

Duvall had an important surveillance job the next day, and I wasn't about to keep him from it.

"Go," I said. "You can't be my full-time babysitter."

"I suppose." He looked reluctant. "I'd put this off if I could, but unfortunately . . . ."

"Please. You have a business to run, and for that matter, so do I. Do what you have to. I'll see you later."

"All right," he said. "Promise me you'll be careful. Stay home today."

"The last time I saw Diesel, he'd broken into my apartment. Maybe that's the wrong thing to do. I should probably go to a library or a coffee shop. Some public place where he won't be able to harm me."

He nodded. "That's a thought. But watch your back."

"Don't worry, Dad. I won't take any candy from strangers."

My dismissive remark made him smile, but did little to calm my own nerves.

φφφ

After Duvall left, I called the attorney in my "bruised knee" case. He made it sound like we were on the road to a settlement. Then I called Sheila to check on my mail. In addition to the usual bills and junk, a couple of things from the court clerk and an oversized envelope from Slippery Steve awaited my return. He'd probably sent something to placate me. Whether it was enough, remained to be seen.

I breathed a sigh of relief. Things seemed to be looking up.

I stopped at the office to fetch the mail and went to the Starbucks where I'd been working lately. As I bought my "grande" Italian Roast, I felt a twinge of guilt about giving my money to "Big Coffee" instead of my favorite neighborhood coffee shop, but Starbucks had wi-fi access.

I was reviewing the answers to interrogatories Slippery Steve had sent when my phone rang. The number was blocked, but I answered anyway.

"Hello, Ms. McRae." The voice was deep, with a hint of menace.

"Who is this?" I asked, though I was pretty sure I knew.

"I should feel offended that you don't remember me, chickie-poo. Of course, we didn't meet under the happiest circumstances, did we?"

Diesel. How had he gotten my cell number? Duh! My calls were still being forwarded from the office. Checking my assumption, I asked, "How did you get this number?" I forced my voice to stay low and calm.

"You're listed in the phone book, aren't you? Anyway, a friend of yours has your card. Perhaps you'd like to speak to her." There was a pause, then I heard Tina. "Sam," she said, in a quavering voice. "This man . . . he come to the motel and made me leave wit' him."

"Tina, are you okay?"

"I'm all right, but I wanna go home. I wanna see my pops."

Her tone was full of naked fear. I didn't have the heart to tell her that her uncle had killed her father.

"Tina, don't panic. The man won't hurt you if you go along with him." I hoped to God this was true. When I heard no response, I said, "Tina? Tina, are you there?"

"Excellent advice, Ms. McRae. I keep telling little Tina that if she'll simply behave, everything will go fine. Now, if you'll behave, too, we'll all be happy."

I'd had enough of this psycho-bully's verbal fencing. "What do you want?" I said, with a steely confidence I didn't feel.

"That delightful landlady of Cooper's told me you came by and copied some of his paperwork, including his calendar and the ITN invoices. I want you to give me your copies of that information, along with all the information you got from that private eye in Philadelphia. Now don't lie to me—I know the contents of that box were sent to you."

"And if I don't?"

"Then you won't be seeing your little friend alive again."

The evidence from Cooper's room, which I had yet to take to the cops, linked Cooper to the embezzlement; and the calendar linked Cooper with Diesel and Powell. Apparently, Diesel didn't realize the cops had other evidence of his involvement. As long as he didn't know that, I could negotiate for Tina's release.

"Okay," I said. "How do we work this?"

"Bring all the documents to Calvert Road Park in half an hour," he said. "I believe you know where that is."

The phone went dead.

CHAPTER THIRTY-ONE

Twenty-five minutes later I sat in my car at Calvert Road Park, clutching the file as I waited for the black compact to appear.

I had the radio on low. I could make out Billy Joe Armstrong of Green Day singing a request that someone wake him up when September ended. I was beginning to feel that way about October. The last couple of weeks had passed slowly as molasses. I glanced at my watch and looked around the parking lot. No other cars. Nothing to duck behind, not in the lot anyway. I swiveled round to scan the trees behind me. At one end of the lot were restrooms in a nondescript building with a shabby forest-green roof.

I didn't see anyone. I tried to calm myself by singing along with Billy Joe.

I watched a black car reach the entrance and turn into the lot.

"Summer has come and passed," I sang. "The innocent can never last . . . ."

The car pulled in front of mine. Diesel was behind the wheel. I could see the top of Tina's head. She slouched in the passenger seat.

"Wake me up . . . when October ends," I took some poetic license with the words and turned off the radio. I opened the door and slid out with the file. Diesel emerged from the black car, unfolding his bulk until he stood looking as friendly as a blond grizzly bear.

Holding the file up for inspection, I said, "Here it is. Is Tina all right?"

He raised his chin a fraction in acknowledgment, then reached into the car and yanked Tina out by her arm. Holding her tight to him, he walked her around the back of his car.

Tina looked terrified, but unharmed. I stepped a few feet from my car and waited. As he approached, he pulled a gun from under his jacket and pressed the barrel against Tina's temple. She whimpered and sniffled, her face wet with tears. I focused on appearing confident, in charge. I tried to convey my false confidence to Tina by looking her in the eye and thinking, *It'll be all right . . . it'll be all right.*

"I hope that's all of it," he said.

I nodded and moved a little to his left, slowly. "I can show you, if you like."

Diesel pivoted. He faced me, Tina held in front of him as a shield. "Of course, I like," he said, the scorn plain in his voice. "I want to see it all."

He moved closer. I stepped back.

"Can I put this on your trunk?"

He nodded and I moved toward his car, placing the file on it and fiddling with the contents. Diesel kept rotating so I was always in his line of sight. I made sure not to stand directly in front of him.

Now would be nice, I thought.

As if I'd willed it to happen, two popping sounds came from the woods. Diesel lurched and stiffened, blood spraying from two holes, one on each side of his chest. And inches from Tina's head. He moaned as his arms went lax. Tina managed to wriggle free before he collapsed to the pavement. She ran to me, sobbing, and threw her arms around me. I hugged her and said, "It'll be okay now."

Little D emerged from behind the building and walked over, gripping a handgun with a long-barreled silencer, and picked up Diesel's gun. "Nice job," he said. "You got him in exactly the right place for me to take my shots." He gestured toward the bathrooms.

I didn't say anything. I didn't want to think about what we'd done.

Little D checked the compact's ignition. "Ah-ight. Keys still here." He got in and started it, pulling it forward a few feet to allow me to leave. He switched off the motor and got out.

"You gots to go now," he said.

"Thanks for coming, D," I said. I looked at Diesel, who lay twitching and prone on the pavement, his breathing labored. "What . . . .?"

"Don't ask," he said.

Tina was still crying softly, clinging to me like a life raft. I disengaged myself from her grasp, while keeping an arm around her shoulder, and led her to my car. We got in and drove away, without looking back.

φφφ

Thirty minutes hadn't given me much time to prepare, but it was just enough to make some calls and run to the office for the file. I'd tried calling CID and couldn't reach a detective. Rather than waste precious time on police bureaucracy, I'd hung up and called Little D.

He said he would park far from the meeting place and approach the lot from the woods. He assured me he could make it. I didn't know he had until I heard the shots.

We hadn't discussed what would happen. And I hadn't given it much thought. As I drove off with Tina beside me, I was struck by my lack of concern that Diesel was a dead man. Seemed like I should feel guilty, but I felt only relief, sweet relief.

CHAPTER THIRTY-TWO

I took Tina to CID, where Powell was being interrogated. Turning my evidence over to Detective Harris, I waited with Tina while arrangements were made to put her in emergency shelter care.

Harris told me the police asked Mrs. Mallory, Shanae's next-door neighbor, to come in. Maybe she could identify Powell as the person she saw leaving the house the night Shanae was killed. Powell was slight and light-skinned. In the right clothes, he could have passed for a gawky teenager. They would check the phone records, to see if he had placed a call to Shanae's house or vice versa.

When they told Tina about her uncle and her father, she showed little emotion. I had expected more tears or rage, but I think the child had shut down. She was past the point of feeling further pain. She stared, in an almost catatonic state, as we waited. When an officer came for her, I asked for five minutes. I crouched beside Tina.

"Tina," I said, handing her my card again. "You know you can call me, any time, if you ever want to talk."

"Why he do it?" she asked. "Why Mr. Powell kill my moms?"

"He was involved in something that would have gotten him in big trouble. He would have lost his job, gone to prison. When your mom found out about Greg, it was only a matter of time before Mr. Powell would have been found out."

"But why he set me up? What I do to him?"

I paused. "I don't know. I guess he knew you and your mom didn't get along. He knew you were associated with a gang. And he knew how girl gangs operate. I don't think he was trying to pin it on you. Any girl in the gang would do." I wasn't sure I believed it. Or that Tina believed it either.

She backhanded the tears off her cheeks. I handed her a tissue and she blew her nose. "What's going to happen?"

"They'll find you a place to live. A group home, probably."

"A foster home."

"Yes."

"So now I ain't got nobody. Not even my pops or my uncle."

"You have me."

She gave me a funny look.

"I lost my parents when I was nine," I said. "I had a cousin who took me in, but I learned to rely on myself a lot. I learned to trust my instincts. And I learned how to take care of myself. You can learn too. If you ever have a problem you feel you can't handle alone, you can call me and talk about it."

"You saved my life," she said. "But you ain't my kin."

"No, but neither are these gangbangers you've been running with. And they're not going to lead you anywhere good."

I could have said that her mother had been kin, for all the good she'd done Tina. I didn't. Some things are best left unsaid.

I told her that, no matter where she went, she was never alone as long as she had good friends to turn to. I told her to respect herself and make the kind of friends who respected themselves and her. There was more I wanted to say, but it didn't seem like the right time. And I couldn't be sure Tina understood all of it. When the officer came to take her, I felt a sense of loss over this girl I'd barely begun to know. I knew she faced an uncertain future. There were probably no big family dinners and white picket fences where she was going. She held her own fate in her hands. Or did she? I've often wondered what causes one person to succeed and another to fail. How much is in our own hands? Are some of us born with two strikes against us from the very beginning?

 φφφ

Tina was represented by a private attorney who handled a lot of pro bono CINA—or "children in need of assistance"— cases. On occasion, we would talk about her. It looked like I might end up as a witness in the case. I felt too emotional about Tina's situation to make an effective advocate. Having counsel who specialized in CINA cases seemed to be in her best interest. She ended up in a shelter home, but I don't know where it is. She hasn't called since I last saw her. At least, not yet. I hope we'll talk again, after she's had time to sort things out. She needs to be the one to decide when that is.

Kozmik confirmed that the computers had been tampered with, but the work station couldn't be identified. It was never established if Saltzman or LaRue, the game developers, or Fullbright, their boss, had done it. The old data were recovered. They revealed that the account had been set up before Brad started working at Kozmik. He was off the hook. There was insufficient evidence to indicate who had taken the money. The cops were unable to turn up child porn on any of the suspects' computers.

Based on the evidence, I was able to clear Brad of the murder charges.

When Brad was exonerated, the Higgins family had a party after Walt was released from the hospital. Walt, a few friends and relatives, and I attended. After dinner Brad wowed us with a slideshow on his new laptop—pictures of a trip he had taken the previous year to the Tetons. He awed the guests with his digital deftness—enhancing images, playing with the colors, sharpening contrast, and zooming in on faraway objects.

Afterward, when the guests went to the dining room for cake and coffee, I hung around while he packed up his laptop. "You're good at working with digital photographs," I said.

"I told you. I like computers."

"As I recall, you said you particularly like computer games, right?"

"Right." He stuck the laptop in its carrying case. "I think it would be fun to create them for a living."

"Were you involved in creating new games with Chip Saltzman and Mike LaRue?"

He gave me a blank look. "Huh?"

"The child porn images. The cops never found them on their computers. They must have used someone else's equipment."

"What makes you think they used mine?"

"Our private investigator. It took a while to get the latest data, but your bank records showed an unusual increase in your savings account, a couple of months before you were accused of embezzlement." I looked at him. "You didn't embezzle that money, did you? But the embezzlers paid you for the use of your sophisticated computer equipment."

"Of course not. My parents gave me that money."

"That should be easy to confirm. I'll ask them right now."

"No!" Brad said, sharply. "Don't bother." He zipped up the carrying case.

"You had to get it from somewhere. I remembered that you had expressed an interest in computer gaming and starting your own business. It occurred to me that maybe Fullbright, Saltzman, and LaRue weren't the only ones involved in making the child porn game, even if they were the only ones taking money from the company."

Brad turned away, wearing a sly smile.

"How did you get in on it?"

"I overheard them talking about it, after hours," he said. "They were talking about setting up an interactive adult entertainment game. They were worried about using the equipment at work because it would leave a record on the computers. They knew they'd get fired in a heartbeat for misusing the equipment and working on pornographic games. At the time, I didn't realize they were talking about kids." He shook his head, in a manner that struck me as disingenuous. "Anyway, I let them know I'd heard them. I told them I wanted in, or I'd tell on them. That freaked them out. I certainly see why now. They paid me for my silence and used my equipment. They even taught me a few programming tricks in the bargain. It was a nice arrangement." He shrugged. "I didn't know they were embezzling from the company to subsidize this. Everything I said about that was true."

"So nothing ever showed up on their computers," I said. "Or would show up on yours, I'd wager. I see you have a new laptop."

"Sometimes it's best to cut your losses and run," he said. "Even if I had the photos on my computer, you can't turn me in. You're my lawyer. And I have the right to remain silent."

"Well, your co-workers' little side project almost got me and your devoted uncle killed," I said.

"That's because you were investigating the embezzlement," he said. He dropped his voice and emphasized his words. "I didn't know anything about the child porn. I swear!"

"One was tied to the other," I said, my voice calm and steady, belying the rage I felt. "As far as I'm concerned, the blood of everyone who died for this is on your hands, too."

Brad said nothing, exercising his right to remain silent. He remains silent to this day. As do I. I didn't tell Walt. As I say, some things are best left unsaid.

φφφ

Whether Powell will go down for Shanae's murder remains to be seen. The evidence I gave them is thin. Although her description matches Powell, and the prosecution can call her as a witness, Mrs. Mallory wasn't sure he was the one she saw that night at Shanae's house. Other than Cooper's calendar and the photos, no one can connect Powell with the child porn operation or Kozmik. Beaufort or Fisher could have, if they'd lived, which leads me to believe Beaufort's "suicide" was anything but. If Powell keeps his mouth shut, and the defense attorney can discredit Mrs. Mallory on cross-examination, he may get away with murder. In any case, I suspect I have no further worries. Thanks to Little D, Diesel's gone for good. He won't be missed.

I guess you could say everything worked out okay in the end. As okay as it could under the circumstances. There are some things that simply can't be fixed. I can't fix the system, I can't fix society, and I can't solve everyone's problems. But I do what I can. The chips fall where they do. At least I can look in the mirror and say I tried. And that's okay.

ABOUT THE AUTHOR

Debbi Mack has published one other novel, *Identity Crisis*, the first Sam McRae mystery. She's also published *Five Uneasy Pieces*, a short story collection that includes her Derringer Award–nominated story "The Right to Remain Silent," originally published in 2009 in *The Back Alley Webzine*. Her work has appeared in the anthologies *Chesapeake Crimes* and *Chesapeake Crimes: They Had It Comin'*.

A former attorney, Debbi has also worked as a journalist, reference librarian, and freelance writer/researcher. She's currently working on the next Sam McRae novel and other projects.

CPSIA information can be obtained
at www.ICGtesting.com
Printed in the USA
FFOW03n1925230115
10476FF